THE DEADLY PUB QUIZ

Abigail Summers Cozy Mysteries
Book 2

ANN PARKER

Copyright © 2024 Ann Parker

Layout design and Copyright © 2024 by Next Chapter

Published 2024 by Next Chapter

Cover art by Lordan June Pinote

This book is a work of fiction. Names, characters, places, and incidents are the product of the author's imagination or are used fictitiously. Any resemblance to actual events, locales, or persons, living or dead, is purely coincidental.

All rights reserved. No part of this book may be reproduced or transmitted in any form or by any means, electronic or mechanical, including photocopying, recording, or by any information storage and retrieval system, without the author's permission.

*Dedicated to my wonderful husband, Terry,
who has been suffering from Parkinson's Disease
for years and never complains.
Throughout all his pain, he has always encouraged me to
follow my dream and keep writing.*

Dora Bream is a creature of habit. Every day she gets up at six-thirty and has a cup of tea with two biscuits. On a Sunday, she attends St. Mary's Church in Becklesfield. Monday is Women's Institute day, and Wednesday morning she visits the library to exchange her romance novels. On a Friday, she takes the nine o'clock bus to Gorebridge, then orders a pot of tea for one in the Willow Tea Room, followed by the short walk to the Home Counties National Bank, where she deposits her blackmail takings for the previous week.

Chapter 1

"I really can't remember the last time Mrs Bream missed church, can you, Mrs Hobbs?" asked a tall, thin elderly lady.

A short, plump elderly lady answered her. "No, Mrs Dawkins, I cannot. It would be awful if something has happened. The service just wasn't the same without her."

"I know, Mrs Hobbs. It was marvellous," and they both giggled.

"I'd be so upset, I'd have to drown my sorrows in champagne," she chuckled. "And she did the flowers so beautifully this week." They both looked at the large display on a wooden pedestal, to the right of the altar. "Dahlias, roses and lilies, straight from her garden."

Mrs Dawkins tutted. "Mind you, I thought everyone knew that yellow roses are unlucky."

"My mother always said, 'A lily and a yellow rose, out the window good luck goes'. You would have thought her coven would have told her that," which set them off again until they remembered where they were.

"I'm sure she's fine. The devil takes care of his own."

"I expect you're right. Maybe her broomstick broke down," whispered Mrs Hobbs, giggling.

"Perhaps the vicar will let someone else do the flowers for a change. I swear he lets her get away with murder." Shirley Dawkins had been trying to have her turn since the last Harvest Festival.

They left the wooden pews and went up the aisle to the back of the church, where they added their hymn books to the pile. They joined the queue at the door to thank the young Reverend Pete Stevens for his excellent service, even though Shirley Dawkins' aching bones were telling her it was a bit on the long side.

Mrs Hobbs pushed in front of her friend. "We were just saying, Reverend, that it's most unusual for Mrs Bream to miss church. We're both rather worried. Do you think she's alright?"

"I'm sure she's fine. She looked very well yesterday when she did the flower arrangements. She said something about expecting company when she left, so maybe they stayed over. Mary will be seeing her for the WI meeting at the vicarage tomorrow, but to put your minds at ease, I'll pop over later to check on her. After my dinner, though. We're having roast beef and Yorkshire pudding at one, and Mary will shoot me if I'm late."

"I'm very grateful, thank you. We would be so upset if anything had happened to our dear friend," said Mrs Hobbs, as she walked away so the vicar did not see the wicked look in her eye and the smile on her face.

This left it to Mrs Dawkins to add, "And thank you for the wonderful service, Vicar."

So it was that on Sunday afternoon, after a huge plate of roast beef and all the trimmings, followed by rhubarb crumble and custard, Pete Stevens and his wife, Mary, reluctantly walked up the path to Dora Bream's large, imposing house on the edge of the village green. Mary looked at the immaculate front garden and wondered why the vicarage's garden always had more weeds than actual flowers, whereas there was not one on show at Dora's. Pete pressed the doorbell as his wife frowned. "I suppose she is alright. It isn't like her to miss a chance to gossip."

"Sshh. She's not deaf."

"You can say that again. She makes out she is, you know, but if someone dropped a pin on the other side of the road, she'd hear it well enough. I happened to mention to Mrs Fish that someone had broken into the Major's, and she piped up from the other end of the church, wanting to know who did what when? Not that we knew anything ourselves, we had just seen the police there. Anyway, no one's in. Let's go home, darling, and snuggle on the sofa and let our dinner go down."

"Good idea. But we'd better check round the back in case she's fallen in the garden or something." They followed the path round to the large landscaped garden, calling out for Dora as they went. The curtains were open so they knew she wasn't still in bed. They tapped on the French window and, when nothing was heard, they tried the brass handle and walked in.

"Dora, are you home? It's Pete and Mary. We were worried when you didn't come to church today." There was no sign of anyone being there until they reached the chintz-covered sofa, where Mary forgot for a second that she was the vicar's wife and screamed out two very rude words. From behind it, protruded a pair of stockinged legs with red, fur-lined slippers. They had found the missing Dora.

Detective Chief Inspector Johnson was miserable at the best of times, but today was Sunday, and he had been on his third pint at the Red Lion in Gorebridge when his sergeant, Dave Mills, had phoned him. He nearly drove to Becklesfield himself but decided to get a lift with him. Just be his luck if he got caught drinking and driving. Mills still had to wait outside for half an hour while his boss finished his pint and had a whisky chaser.

"Can't even have a day off on a Sunday now. Not exactly a 999 call, is it?" asked the grumpy inspector. "Some old biddy, I heard."

"If you mean an elderly woman, yes, you're right, Sir. But I think you'll find it was worth an emergency call. You'll see what I mean."

"Pension book missing, is it?" scoffed Johnson.

"Not quite, Sir. A Mrs Dora Bream was found by the local vicar and his wife, strangled to death with a silk scarf."

Chapter 2

THE MEMBERS OF THE DEADLY DETECTIVE AGENCY IN Becklesfield were taking a much-needed day off. After the success of 'The Case of the Hospital Homicides', as Abigail called it, they had been run off their feet. Not that their success had been advertised in The Chiltern Weekly. That would have been rather difficult as the said agency was a group of dearly departeds, of which Abigail Summers was the self-appointed leader. Not only because she had a brilliant mind for solving puzzles, but mainly because she was bossy and liked to be in charge. There was another member who was very much alive - Abigail's friend, Hayley, a psychic who, luckily for them, happened to be married to a policeman named Tom.

When thirty-nine year-old Abigail had first died and found out that she had been murdered, she asked for help from a group of also-deads, who hung out in the local library. At that time, they were led by Terry Styles, a handsome, but grumpy, middle-aged man. He loved and hated Abigail in equal measure, although love was edging in front as time went by. Her blue eyes, beguiling smile, and sense of humour helped. It had been her idea to start the agency, after they solved her murder. She wanted to name it after herself, but they already thought she was big-headed enough, after solving the case before the police did, so they all settled for The Deadly Detective Agency.

As it was a Sunday, and it was closed to the public, they were lazing about in their local haunt, the Becklesfield Public Library in the High Street. There was Suzie, a young black girl, and her guardian in the afterlife, Lillian Yin, who was still dressed in her nurse's uniform. The mother of the group was amiable, eighty-two-year-old, wannabe sleuth, Betty, who was having the time of her life since being dead.

Abigail felt fed up and was pacing up and down. The detective agency was the most exciting thing that she had done. She had been a dressmaker who ran her own sewing business for all her working life and was beginning to wish she had joined the police when she'd had her chance. Although she would have wanted to go straight into CID, of course. She loved a good mystery or, better still, a good murder.

"For goodness' sake, sit down," said Terry. "It is rest in peace, you know. We said we would have a crime-free day today. In fact, it was your idea to not investigate on a Sunday."

"I don't think so. Oh yeah, it was me. But that was because we closed two major cases last week." They had worked out that a jealous husband had killed a tennis professional in 1938 at Chiltern Hall, and their other success was rounding up a kidnapping gang and releasing the hostage. But rather than it being a drug cartel from nearby Gorebridge, it had been a group of nine and ten-year-olds from the village, and the victim was a garden gnome. The miscreants were brought to justice and given a one-week suspended grounding. But a win was a win, thought Abigail, so it seemed like a good idea at the time to give themselves a day off.

"But now I'm bored stiff. Sorry, another unintended pun. We need a good old-fashioned murder. Failing that, I say we all go for a walk on Chittering Downs. It's a perfect summer's day."

"I'd love that," said Suzie. "Come on, Lillian. Can Tiggy come?"

"Of course," said Abigail. Tiggy was a ginger cat that had found Abigail and led her to her kitten that she had given birth to in the graveyard before she had died. Luckily for the tiny bundle of fur, Abigail had managed to get her friend and fellow agent, psychic medium Hayley, to rescue the near-dead kitten and nurse it back to health.

They couldn't have solved the mysteries or murders without the help of Hayley Moon, which was her professional name. She was married to Police Constable Tom Bennett, the bane of DCI Johnson's life. He could never work out how he was always in the right place or time to solve the cases. Tom had even impressed the Chief Constable, and so he vowed to bring the young policeman down and find out where he was getting his information from if it killed him. There was a rumour going around that a psychic was helping him and the force, but he didn't believe in that rubbish.

Terry and Betty had no desire to walk up to Chittering Downs, and thought a day of peace and quiet would be much more to their taste. So Suzie, Lillian, Abigail, and a small ginger cat took the path past the church, and around the edge of the village pond to the start of the footpath. It was a lovely, sunny day and the sun shone on Abigail's shoulder-length, wavy blonde hair. They could follow the trail all the way to Great Billings, where Suzie liked watching the gliders being towed up and left to soar above.

But Lillian had a feeling that their hike would be abandoned as soon as she saw police cars and a crowd gathered outside one of the large detached houses on the green. She knew the house well.

"My mother's friend lives there, Dora Bream. Her husband

died years ago and her children, two boys, I think it was, moved away. She's a sweet little thing as long as you don't get on the wrong side of her."

Abigail's eyes lit up when she saw PC Tom standing outside the gate moving the nosy crowd back. "Ooh, I wonder what's happened?"

Lillian knew exactly what she was going to say next, and that their walk would not be going ahead.

"There's only one way to find out. Come on, let's go and have a look."

"Don't get too excited," said Suzie. "She might have just had an accident. Or been burgled."

They all said a polite hello to Tom as they walked past him, but he couldn't see or hear them. His wife, Hayley, was the only one with that ability. They didn't give the same courtesy to grizzled DCI Johnson, who was talking to Sergeant Mills outside the front door. He treated everyone like they were suspects and was none too fussy about who he arrested, as long as he got a result and could get to the pub. The members of the agency knew he hated their friend, Tom Bennett, as he was the favourite of Chief Constable Carson, as not only had the young policeman found a missing child, but he had also saved the life of a female kidnap victim. Johnson had a feeling that his weird, hippy wife had something to do with it and was feeding him information, but he didn't want to be laughed at, so he kept quiet. His long-suffering sergeant, Dave Mills, thought the same but was more than happy to get to the top on Tom's coattails. And he had a lot of time for the friendly and kind-hearted constable. He looked forward to the day when Johnson was given his marching orders and Bennett would be his sergeant. Surely that wouldn't be much longer. The group of three spirits walked past the Vicar and his wife, who were looking nervous, and standing on the path that led to the back garden. Abigail suspected it might have been them that found the body, that was if it was indeed a murder.

The sitting room at Dora's house was filled with a forensic team taking fingerprints and photographs. Lillian told nine-year-old Suzie not to look while she and Abigail walked through those working to look at the body of Dora Bream. Her grey hair, partially covering her face, could not hide the fearful expression. The bulging eyes stared straight up and if it wasn't for the maroon and gold, silk scarf wrapped tightly around her neck, she might have been having a lie-down. Being an ex-nurse, Lillian went to have a closer look.

"Petechiae to both eyes and a red face. Definitely death by strangulation. Poor little thing. It wouldn't have taken long." A sudden flash made Lillian jump up. The police photographer kept snapping, making it impossible to find out anything further, much to the nurse's annoyance. Abigail had been told that even they could show up on cameras or CCTV, so she wondered if they had been caught in the act. That would be very interesting to find out.

"I have a feeling I've seen her somewhere, but I can't think where. What was she like?" she asked.

"I would have thought she was the last person to get murdered. She was an elder at the church for a start, and did the flowers and stuff. Then she ran a lot of charities and volunteered for anything going. My mum said she would get an MBE one day."

Abigail thought hard. "Hmm. Just because they are do-gooders, doesn't mean to say they don't do-bad."

Mills and Johnson tried to enter the room but were sent out by the crime scene investigators, who told them they could come back when they had finished and the body had been taken away for a post-mortem. Unbeknown to them, they were followed into the dining room by the spirits of two ladies, a child, and a cat.

"Was there any sign of a break-in, Mills?"

"No, Sir. But this is the kind of village where people leave their doors open all day. Reverend Stevens said that Dora always had her front and back doors locked but left the French window open so she could go in and out of her garden."

"Huh, where I live in Gorebridge, if I left my window open an inch, I'd come back to an empty house. Didn't do her much good for all that. But then again, she might have been expecting the murderer and invited them in for tea and crumpets."

"There was no sign of that, Sir. But whoever it was might have knocked at the door, and she let them in. The wife would love a dining room like this."

It was magazine-beautiful, with gold and cream Regency wallpaper and pale yellow paintwork. The thick curtains had French pleating at the top and were tied back with gold, tasselled cords. But it was overshadowed by a large, oval walnut table with eight chairs. In the centre was a large, silver candlestick with four white candles, none of which had ever been lit. A sign of a lonely life perhaps, thought Abigail. No evidence either of any dinner parties or family visits. In front of the chair nearest to them, the local paper was spread out, and an eight-inch pair of scissors appeared to have cut into one side of the page and were lying on top.

"What do you make of this, Sir?" asked Mills, pointing to the table.

None of the females present were surprised at Johnson's answer. He wasn't a fan of women in general, or men actually, some thought.

"Who knows what goes on in a woman's mind? She was probably cutting out a recipe or making a pattern for a skirt."

"I haven't noticed a sewing machine, and looking at this room, I wouldn't say that she was big on entertaining."

"Well done, Sergeant Mills. I'm very impressed," said Abigail, not that he could hear.

"A sale coupon then. These rich types are always trying to save a bit of money. Now what's the chance that old Dora put her scarf on and accidentally tripped and it got caught, and she strangled herself?"

"Are you thinking Isadora Duncan, Sir?" asked Mills, who for the first time, was actually impressed with his knowledge.

Johnson rolled his eyes. "Keep up, lad. Her name is Dora, not Isadora, and her surname is Bream, not Duncan. Honestly, the youth of today," he mumbled. Mills didn't bother explaining who he really meant. He wouldn't thank him, and it would be a waste of time. "As soon as the others have gone, get that Bennett in here with you, and I want you to go right through this house, top to bottom. Bag anything important and make sure you both put gloves on." He noticed he had forgotten to put his own on and put his hands in the pockets of his crumpled suit jacket. "Then do a house-to-house. See if she had any visitors last night or this morning."

"Where will you be, Sir?"

"I'll get a lift with one of the uniforms back to Gorebridge and see what my sources can come up with." In other words, thought both Abigail and Mills, he would be at The Red Lion, and the only sauce he'd be seeing today would be on his burger.

Chapter 3

ABIGAIL KNEW THAT BETTY AND TERRY WOULD BE most annoyed if they weren't told about this latest murder, so they ran back to the library to tell them, and then they all made for Hayley's on the other side of the village. They hurried down Church Lane to her house, which was the one with wind chimes and a dreamcatcher hanging in the porch. Young Hayley Bennett had given up on privacy since the day that four ghosts had turned up in her conservatory as she was meditating and had turned her world upside down. Her friend Abigail had been murdered, and they needed her help, as well as a great deal of help from her policeman husband. But it had changed her life for the better, as now she had the chance to put her God-given gift to get peace for some and justice for others. Probably the most important benefit was that now her husband, Tom, no longer doubted or could ignore her supernatural abilities.

Because it was Sunday, she was peeling the potatoes for a late dinner with Tom. She probably wouldn't have bothered, but her husband still wanted his traditional roast dinner, like his mother used to make. She had just got the roasting tin out when she felt the temperature drop and excited voices vying for her attention. She dried her hands and saw her kitchen full of the other detectives. Luna, the tortoiseshell kitten, ran around excitedly when he saw his mother, Tiggy, who had come with them. He had grown stronger every day, and although Tom didn't want to ever have a cat, let alone a feral one, he had stopped calling him 'bloody cat' and spent more time petting or playing with him than she did. And it was funny how Luna was always curled up on her husband's side of the bed by morning.

"Goodness, what's happened?" Hayley Bennett looked over at Terry. "You explain, hun. I can't hear a word of it. Come on, let's go into the garden. Jane, the next-door neighbour, is away for the weekend." She had learned the hard way that communicating with ghosts could get you in trouble for talking and laughing to yourself. She tried to pretend to use her phone or read from a book when she could.

Betty, Lillian, and Abigail sat on the patio chairs with Hayley, while young Suzie sat on the grass and played with the cats. Terry cleared his throat and began. "I've no doubt that you know Dora Bream. Well, she's been murdered in her own home. Strangled."

"Oh no, poor little Dora. Do they know who did it?"

"They…" answered Terry, but Abigail took over. To be honest, he was surprised that she had lasted that long.

"No, they haven't got a clue, Hayley. They have no idea why anyone would want to kill a sweet old lady either. But as you know, someone even killed me."

Terry tutted. "Well, that I can understand."

Abigail just ignored the comment and gave him a dirty look, as the others laughed. "Johnson was there, and now Tom and Sergeant Mills are searching the house and then going door to door."

"I might as well forget our Sunday lunch then. When did it happen? Thinking about it, she wasn't in church today. She often does the reading, but Esme Cove did one today for the first time in ages."

"I've no idea, but Lillian might. She got a good look at the body."

"I don't know for sure, but it didn't look like it had happened in the last, say, twelve hours. There were petechiae in both eyes, red dots, so definitely strangulation. Unfortunately, I couldn't feel her to tell myself, but I heard one of the ladies say that full rigour mortis had set in. So I reckon it was sometime last night."

Abigail wondered if they could work out the time of death. "We were there at about half two and the curtains were all open."

"I just happen to know that she got up very early every day, so they must have been pulled back from the day before. This time of year I close mine about nine o'clock, so we can assume that she died sometime yesterday, maybe in the evening. I'll find out from Tom who saw her last and at what time. So what exactly was she strangled with?"

"It was some kind of silk scarf. Dark red with those fleur-de-lis patterns all over it, in gold. We need to find out if it was hers," said Abigail.

Betty couldn't be silent any longer. She was the most enthusiastic of all the investigators. She had been married to John for sixty years and had died a week after her husband about a year ago, and so she called this her me-time. "But what are we going to do first? We need to start investigating as soon as we can, don't we?"

"Maybe you could help there, Betty. We need to find out exactly what sort of person she was. So far I've heard she's a poor little thing and a do-gooder, but don't get on the wrong side of her. And going by her house, she didn't seem to have a lot of company, so she couldn't have been that likeable. And everyone seems to say poor little Dora. How little was she?"

14

"Not much over five feet as I remember. But don't let that fool you. She was no walkover. I knew her rather well back in the day," said Betty. "She wasn't my idea of fun. She liked bird-watching for a start. A bit snooty as well if you ask me. She did a lot for charity, but I wouldn't have said she was charitable, as such. She volunteered at the charity shop in the high street if they couldn't get anyone."

"Wet & Wildlife? I get most of my long skirts I always wear from them. You can't beat it," said Hayley. "And remember that's how we met, Abi, because you used to have to alter them sometimes."

Abigail nodded and agreed. "I loved that shop. I used to get all my books from there and I could take them back when I'd read them. And I liked that because all the profits go to the local woodlands and rivers. And I love badgers. I might have even seen her there then. No, it wasn't there. I've just realised where I know her from. She comes to the library once a week. Anything else, Betty?"

"You're right, I've seen her in there as well. Now, I think her husband was a civil servant who caught the train to London every day. I'm only guessing but I reckon he died about ten years ago. I think the only time she spoke to me was if she wanted to know something."

Lillian joined in, "You've just reminded me, Betty. I remember my mum and dad laughing about her one day. Apparently, they were in the Cricketers Inn and she was getting her sherry from the bar and asking James Rich, the landlord, all sorts of questions, like had he been married before? Where was he from? What job did he have previously? Where was he born? Did he have children? So he said to her, 'Where are you from, Spain?', and laughed. Well, she looked puzzled and said no, she was half Welsh and she didn't understand until another chap at the bar said that James meant that she was like the Spanish Inquisition, and they all started laughing. So she slammed her glass on the bar and I don't think she went in there ever again."

"So I think we can add nosy as well then," said Abigail. She had been told she was nosy once or twice and she had loved a good gossip when she was alive. Caring and interested in people's problems was how she preferred to see it. "That could well be the motive in this case."

"I'm not one to speak ill of the dead," said Betty. "But she was an annoying lady. Dora had a way of talking to you with a smile and holding eye contact, but after a while you realised that she was pumping you for information. It always started nicely enough, but by the end of it, you would wonder why on earth you had shared all that with her. You'd tell her all sorts of things you hadn't wanted to and felt quite shell-shocked by the time she walked away. My husband called her a very dangerous woman. I often wondered what he meant by that."

"Now we're getting somewhere. She must have asked the wrong question to the wrong person," said Hayley. "Do you know anything about her, Terry? Or more importantly, have you seen her since she was killed?" Terry often met the new Deads, as he called them when they came. He had been greeting them for fifty years if they stayed earth-bound. It was him that found Abigail walking near the church. As he told her, the main reasons for that were sudden death from illness, an accident or murder.

Terry replied, "No to both, I'm afraid. I checked around the village earlier today. We need to go and start finding out what we can. There's a few Deads around I could try. Do you want to come with me, Betty? You might know some of them. We'll get a head start."

"Good idea, Terry. The early bird catches the bush. Let's go, we can't sit around here nilly willy." Betty had a saying for every occasion and it was very rare that she said them correctly, but that was part of her charm.

Hayley smiled kindly at her. "Well, do what you can, hun. I'm going to text Tom and see if he can give me any updates. I know Janette in the library thinks I'm a total nut for talking to myself when I'm there with you, but I'll see if she can tell me anything about Dora and the books she chose. That might give us a bit of a clue."

Abigail got to her feet too. "Good idea, Hayl. Come on Lillian, and you, Suzie, let's go back and have a proper look around Dora's house. Hopefully, the others have all gone. And, Tiggy, you get to stay here."

Chapter 4

SERGEANT DAVE MILLS, HELPED BY POLICE CONSTABLE Tom Bennett, worked methodically, covering the whole house. There was very little to show how Dora Bream spent her time at home. Next to her bed, there was a book entitled 'Loves & Studs', with a sheet of paper as a bookmark. Tom flicked through it and thought it was a bit racy for a seventy-year-old churchgoer. The folded piece of paper was a receipt for a double room in a hotel in Brighton, dated nine years ago. He needed to find out exactly when her husband had died. It could be a romantic keepsake of happier days, hence being in her romance novel. He added it to the other evidence they had collected, like her phone and diary. Unfortunately, it didn't seem like she had a laptop, and there was no internet connection. The diary only had a few villagers' names in it, like the vicar and things to do with her various charities. Tom thought Dora was a very conflicting character. Hayley would have said she was a Gemini. She had 'Loves & Studs' next to her bed upstairs, and the Bible on the table next to her chintz wing-backed chair downstairs.

She was obviously a bird lover, as there was a pair of binoculars on the windowsill, with an opened book entitled 'British Garden Birds'. In the corner of the lounge was an antique writing bureau. Must be worth a fortune, the two policemen thought. It had four drawers down each side, and the writing surface lifted up to reveal a space underneath. The only drawer they couldn't check was the bottom one, as it was locked. They looked for a key but there wasn't one in any of the obvious places. The other drawers held an old passport and various receipts and papers, but nothing of importance; however, they put the contents in separate bags just in case. Mills was so pleased that Johnson had left them to it. He would have got a knife and prised open the locked drawer, with no thought for the piece of history that had stayed in perfect condition for at least two hundred years, but would be ruined after being with Johnson for ten minutes. He would ring a locksmith to come on Monday morning.

They put the sealed bags in the boot and started knocking on the neighbours' doors to see if anyone had seen someone visiting Dora since she had got back from the church on Saturday afternoon. It was decided that Mills would go one way round the village green from Dora's house, and Tom would go the other way and meet in the middle.

Sergeant Mills found the first witness with any information when he reached the beamed Tudor house that was directly opposite Dora's. Mrs Northover was a widow who walked with a stick and was a self-confessed busybody.

"At my age, Sergeant, there's not a lot to do. I'm eighty-six, you know."

"Are you really?"

"I used to love my television, but even that bores me silly now. Unless there's a test match on, of course. Like my late husband, I love my cricket. And my eyes aren't good enough to read, so my only pleasure is sitting in this window and watching the world go by."

"So you might remember who came and went at Dora's yesterday afternoon."

"My marbles may be rolling around, but I've still got them, Sergeant. I saw her going out after lunch and coming home at about quarter to five in the afternoon. She was carrying a shopping bag and had her old, brown leather handbag that she always carried, across her body. I do think that is an awful look. In my day, we used to use a bag as if it was part of our outfit, and we would carry it in the crook of our arms. Not slung across like a school satchel. And if I was going out somewhere nice, I'd make sure it matched my shoes. And they'd be proper court shoes with a two-inch heel." Mills thought he would never get back to his eight-month-old daughter if she didn't stop waffling. "Where were we? Oh yes, I had my high tea then. They don't call it that now, do they? I had a nice ham and cucumber sandwich and a scone with jam. Unfortunately, I have to take my tea in one of those awful mugs now. I can't carry a cup and saucer safely with my stick, and it just doesn't taste the same."

"No? So then what?" asked Mills.

"Well, I drank it, of course."

"No, I mean did you see anything to do with the house opposite?" sighed Mills.

"I'm getting to that. I saw Esme Cove go in the gate at about half-past six."

"Who is that? Was she a friend of Dora?" he said, writing the name down in his notebook.

"Dora didn't have friends. She just knew Esme from various things that go on in the village. Her cleaner, Cassie, and her son went every Friday morning to do her cleaning and the gardening while she was in Gorebridge. And she had acquaintances at the church or the WI, but not friends as such. Her two sons moved away years ago, and I've not seen them since, which is a shame. My own son moved to Australia, and I don't suppose I'll ever get to go. I have no other family. That's not to say Dora didn't have visitors. She had a lot more than me for sure. It's nice for me that you're here, Sergeant. It can get so lonely."

He felt guilty for trying to hurry her up. Perhaps he could ask his wife to visit one day. Now she had finished work to look after the baby, she wouldn't mind at all. "Don't worry today, but can you let us know if she's had any unusual visitors over the last few weeks? Thank you. Now you say Esme went in at half-past six, I don't suppose you saw her leave, did you?"

"It must be your lucky day, because I did. About half an hour later. I can't be any more precise. But I didn't see anyone else after that, mainly because I fell asleep in my chair, and I'm afraid I didn't wake up till it was nearly dark. As I closed my curtains, I did wonder if Dora had gone out, because there are usually lights on over there at that time of night and her curtains were still open."

"That's marvellous. You've been a great help. If you wouldn't mind, can you tell me about Esme Cove?"

"She's the Major's wife, as she likes to remind everyone. She's younger than me, but we both went to Becklesfield Primary School. Esme Tuckett as she was then. Her family had money though. When she got older, she went off to a fancy private school in Brighton as a boarder and we sort of lost touch after that. But when she married Major Roland Cove, she moved back here to the huge house on the edge of the village. It's a rather depressing-looking mansion called Grey Towers. Her family have lived there for centuries, since the Spanish Armada, I think. Roland has left the army now, retired, I expect. But I have a feeling that Dora knew the major quite well in the past, because he used to visit her a lot at one time."

Tom wasn't having quite so much luck, although another policeman may have thought his luck was right in! Six doors down from Dora's, he had been invited in by a beautiful, young blonde, Rebecca Jones, who said she had vital information. He was quickly beginning to regret it. Becks, as she said he should call her, was in her mid-twenties and said her husband was travelling on the continent to Amsterdam and Paris for work and would be away until Wednesday. She turned the huge television off, patted the sofa next to her, and told him to take a seat. He was already wishing he hadn't, mainly because the summer dress she was wearing had a way of gaping at the top and parting at the bottom to show her long, tanned legs. Tom blushed and got out his notebook so he would have somewhere else to look.

"So how well did you know the victim? Was she a friend?"

"Hardly. I feel a bit insulted, Constable. I don't think playing bridge and the WI is my cup of tea. Actually, I prefer Malibu and coke. Would you like to join me?"

"Not while I'm on duty, thank you."

"Does that mean you will when you get off?"

"Goodness, no," said a worried Tom. "I'm happily married."

"So am I. Although Mark is never here. I think he only married me for eye candy at the golf club. God, I hate this village. Full of nosy neighbours and boring housewives who hate me." Rebecca went and poured herself a large drink. She sat back down on the sofa and tucked her legs underneath her provocatively.

"So what is the vital information you have, Mrs Jones?"

"Becks please. It's probably not that vital, if I'm honest, but I did see Dora and Major Cove having an awful argument the other day near the Post Office, and he actually grabbed her arm at one point. It was the most exciting thing that has happened lately. I didn't catch what they were saying, although it wasn't for the want of trying."

"What day was that?"

"Let me see….either Tuesday or Wednesday, probably Wednesday, actually. I don't normally shop at the Village Stores, but I had run out of coffee or something boring, so I had to go there."

"We think Mrs Bream was murdered last evening, so we're asking if anyone saw her after half-past four or saw anyone near her house."

"I didn't notice her. A few older kids went by on their bikes. But there were a few that walked past my window around that time. No strangers or anything. You can set your clock by the boring folks around here. There were the usual shopkeepers going home after they had locked up. Mrs. Merry, who owns the florist's, was the first. Being Saturday, Miss Spittle had closed the Post Office at lunchtime. Umm… Julian Banning, who owns the antique shop, walked past, a bit later than usual, it was more like sevenish. But there could have been others. It's not like I'm a nosy neighbour myself. Give me your phone number, and I can ring you if I remember anyone else."

"Er, you can ring the Gorebridge Police Station and ask for DCI Johnson; I'm sure he will be pleased to hear from you," said Tom, getting to his feet.

"Are you sure you can't stay a bit longer, Police Constable Bennett? There is a murderer on the loose, and I am a defenceless woman."

Tom wasn't sure that was true. He was the one that felt defenceless. "I'm sure you will be fine, Mrs. Jones," he said as he made his escape. He knew what the saying 'hot under the collar' meant now. Phew.

Dave Mills was walking towards him as he left and asked, "Did you find out or see anything?"

"Quite a bit of the lady in there," he laughed. "But I'll stick to what she said about the case. She saw Julian Banning, the antique guy, and Mrs Merry walk past early evening, and last Wednesday, she saw Dora having an argument with Major Cove outside the Post Office. Now, last week, I got a call out to a major's house that had been broken into. I have a feeling it might have been him."

"I got his name from someone as well, so that will keep

Johnson happy. And his wife, Esme, was seen visiting Dora at six-thirty. Mrs Northover at Prune Tree Cottage was very helpful and gave me a bit of background about Dora, not all of it useful. Like she said she saw her going home at… Blimey, I've just thought of something."

"To do with her?"

"Yes. She said that Dora always had an old, brown leather bag with her. But I can't remember one, can you?"

"Not unless the forensics took it," said Tom.

"They would have said. That's something else for the boss then. Why don't we call it a day, Tom? We can write up our notes in the morning. Johnson will want to interview the Coves himself anyway, and I want to get back to see Isabella and the baby before she goes to sleep."

"Good idea. Thanks, Serge. I'll see you in the morning." Tom knew his day wouldn't be over. He had a feeling his wife, Hayley, would want all the information for her amateur sleuths. But he couldn't complain; they had helped him get noticed on the force more than once. The only part he didn't like was when they were in his house with Hayley. It was very disconcerting when your wife was talking to ghosts and you didn't know what they were saying.

But that wasn't his worry tonight as he put his key in the front door. After what had happened at Rebecca Jones' house, he was just hoping that with all the supernatural gifts that his wife possessed, she couldn't read minds!

Chapter 5

MATTHEW RIDER WAS GETTING MORE AND MORE worried as time went on. He had been standing looking out of the window ever since he had got up. Where was Lucy? He had never woken up and found she wasn't beside him. And she always rang him when she was going to be late home from work at the office. He couldn't remember any point in the five years of their marriage when she had kept a secret from him, and she had certainly never gone missing before.

"Where are you, Lucy?" he said out loud.

Matthew sat down on a dining room chair and pulled it nearer the window. A few people walked past, but no one looked his way. He had heard a police siren earlier, but that had gone roaring up the lane. He was getting hungry; he hadn't eaten much since six o'clock yesterday when she hadn't got home. He would have a coffee and a biscuit to tide him over. Lucy would be back home soon, and they could eat together. She'd probably be tired, so he'd walk up and get her fish and chips. Or maybe they could go to the Cricketers, just for a quick meal, and then home again.

Perhaps she had missed the last bus back from Gorebridge and stayed with somebody. She was very popular. He had tried to ring all her friends yesterday, but couldn't get hold of anyone. This morning, he had phoned where she worked and was told she wasn't there.

He had a low moment and wondered if she had met someone else and left him. So he checked her wardrobe, but all her things were still there. Her wash things and toothbrush were still in the bathroom, and he picked up her hairbrush off the chest of drawers. It reminded him of her lovely, long auburn hair. That was the first thing that had caught his eye when he first saw her in the art gallery in London.

"It only seems like yesterday to me, Luce. I asked you if you wanted to go for a coffee, and I was so surprised when you said yes. Afterwards, we had a long walk in Regent's Park, until it started to rain, and then we agreed to meet the next day. I couldn't believe it when you actually turned up. Wasn't long before we were married, at that little church where your parents live. What was the name of that village? I forget now. But I'll never forget how beautiful you looked that day. What I'd give to hold you now. I've woken up every day since then and thought how lucky I am."

Matthew still caught men looking at her. He didn't mind; she was beautiful, and he liked them to know that she was with him, and had chosen him from all the others.

He tried to think if there was any clue that she was unhappy. No, they loved each other. There was no doubt. She was always happy to get home from work, and they would sit and watch television together. They never used the dining table these days and ate from trays on their laps. Lucy never was one for going out, unless it was to the local pub, and they would have a meal. Any chance to save cooking. She never had liked that much. He laid down the brush gently and said, "If anyone's touched a hair on your head, sweetheart, I'll kill them." Perhaps he should ring the police. Was she a missing person yet, he wondered.

He hurried downstairs when he thought he heard her come in the door, but it was just a leaflet for pizza. Like he wanted to eat! He went to the window and took up his vigil again. Lucy will be home soon, he told himself.

Chapter 6

ABIGAIL, ALONG WITH LILLIAN AND SUZIE, HAD walked through the yellow crime scene tape surrounding the property to search the victim's house for themselves.

"What I would have given for a house like this," said Lillian. "These two rooms are as big as my flat was."

Suzie looked out of the window into the back garden. "It's big enough for a tennis court out there."

"I wonder who will inherit it. That's motive for killing her alone. It must be worth millions. I would be tempted," laughed Abigail. She'd had a lovely house herself in the village. It hurt to think that someone else lived in it now, even if it was inherited by her nephew.

"She had two boys, but I don't see any photos of them anywhere. I'm sure they got married and had kids, so it's strange that there are no grandchildren's school photographs on the side." They could see a framed black-and-white photograph of their wedding on the mantelpiece and a later one, in colour, of one of their anniversaries. They looked so happy, and Lillian thought it must have been very hard for Dora when her husband died.

"We'll have to get Hayley to find out from Tom where the sons are now and if they were in the area yesterday. Suzie, can you have a good rummage around? We'll start in her bedroom," said Abigail.

Suzie was the only one that could move things. She put her talent down to her being only nine years old, and it was very useful, not only for investigations and looking things up but also for haunting. Abigail had been very pleased when Suzie could pay her nephew back by tipping a vase of flowers into his lap. Aaron had been far too happy to have inherited her house in the will, and showed little emotion that his only aunt had been brutally murdered.

Suzie started by going through her dressing table drawers. "Pretty much as I thought," said Lillian. "Large pants and thick vests." Abigail noted she had a pair of pants just like those, but she decided not to share that fact. However, hidden under a wide-brimmed hat, in a large circular box in the wardrobe, they had quite the shock.

"Oh my, Dora, you little vixen," said Abigail. "She had a better social life than me by the looks of it. You'd better not see this, Suzie."

"I'll have to, and I'm not a baby, you know. What on earth is all this lot? You need me to lift it out anyway. Here goes - handcuffs, black stockings, a plastic whip, and... I've no idea what that is,"

"That is the worst kind of torture, Suzie. I remember it well. It's called a suspender belt and holds up your stockings with those clip things. Thank goodness the girls of today have more sense than wearing them for a man. There's no other reason I can think of for putting one of them on. What else have we got?"

"A very long pair of plastic, black boots," she answered. "Did she have very long legs?" Suzie asked innocently.

Lillian patted her on the head and said, "No, darling. They are over-the-knee PVC boots. They're supposed to be sexy."

"Really? It's all a mystery to me."

"So are we thinking that Dora was the oldest swinger in town, or are these from her younger days?"

"I'm hoping for the latter, if I'm honest," said Lillian.

"Me too. But good on her if she was still up for it. To be honest, even at thirty-nine, I found I would rather go to bed with a hot chocolate and a good mystery book than do all that."

"All what?" asked Suzie.

"Er, well, some people like to play games in bed. You know, like er... ludo or cards. Umm, watch TV, that kind of thing."

"Oh," said Suzie, mischievously. "I thought you were talking about sex," and she started to laugh.

The other two bedrooms showed no signs of anyone using them since Dora's children had left home, so they returned downstairs and looked around the sitting room again. The Crime Scene Investigators had left a mixture of fingerprint powder and rubbish. There was an antique writing bureau, and all the drawers were open and had been emptied. Suzie tried to open the bottom one, but it was locked. It looked like the police and forensics had all done their jobs, as there was nothing of interest. Although Abigail did wonder why the binoculars were on the window sill overlooking the village green, rather than the back garden where the bird feeders were, if Dora was that interested in birdwatching.

The kitchen looked like it had been thoroughly searched as well. They checked every cupboard and drawer just in case. On top of the fridge was a wicker basket that held circulars, which Suzie lifted down. She spread them out on the counter. There was a leaflet for a garden centre and a pizza coupon - two for one. Ooh, I fancy a pizza, thought Abigail. Mmm, pepperami. A stick of paper glue. A menu for a takeaway in Gorebridge and a handwritten note.

"This is probably her writing. It's a list of names who have donated to the Amber Road Bird Sanctuary. Remember these names, you two. There's
J. Rich
C. Briggs
M. Jones
R. Cove
There's no date on it."

"I recognise two of them," said Lillian. "James Rich, the landlord of the Cricketers, and Major Roland Cove."

Abigail knew C. Briggs. "That's Cassie. We went to school together. I think she does a bit of cleaning around the village now. Hayley might be able to tell us who M. Jones is."

At the bottom of the basket was a felt, handmade needle and pin book. It made Abigail a bit sad. In life, if she wasn't sewing something, she was crocheting or knitting. "Aww, I made one of these for my mum when I was about your age, Suzie. I've still got it. Well, I did, but no doubt my nephew has thrown it out by now. Open it up for me, will you, please? Well, mine didn't have one of those in."

Hidden inside was a small key. The perfect size for a drawer in an antique writing desk. Uncharacteristically, Abigail said, "We'll leave it here and tell Tom where to find it. We shouldn't disturb too much evidence. There could be anything in that drawer. Let's see if they have left anything else for us to find."

They went into the dining room and were surprised to see the local newspaper and the scissors still on the table. The police had obviously not thought it was a clue, but Abigail didn't agree and couldn't wait to see what it was on there that was such an interest to Dora.

"Suzie, can you help me read both sides of the page and see what she was about to cut out? I don't think for a minute that it was for a recipe or a skirt pattern like Johnson says. You lift it, and I'll read it out. Lillian, make sure you are listening, in case I forget.

Right, there's been a fatal accident on Devils Hill again. A sale at Hardings Department Store in Gorebridge. Aww, I used to love shopping there. An article about yet another robbery of the rich and famous, this time at Cadderly Manor. Um, there's a man from Little Frimble who won the lottery. An advert about a pub quiz that's on at the Cricketers in Becklesfield on the twenty-seventh. And uh-oh, Hayley is not going to like this one bit!"

Chapter 7

TOM NEED NOT HAVE WORRIED THAT HIS WIFE, Hayley, was going to read his thoughts and know that he had been sitting in close proximity to a gorgeous, young twenty-something. Just as well, because she looked mad as hell.

"Have you read the local paper?" she shouted, which was unusual for her. "I've just seen this."

"Hello to you too. As if I've had time. Why, what's happened?"

"Listen to this advert, Tom.

IS THERE SOMEONE YOU WANT TO REACH?
I CAN HELP YOU TALK TO YOUR LOVED ONES WHO HAVE PASSED
STAR CHARTS AND PALM READINGS
TAROT CARDS
SPIRITUALIST MEETINGS
Contact CLAIRE VOYANT
PROFESSIONAL PSYCHIC MEDIUM
FAMOUS CONSULTANT TO THE GOREBRIDGE POLICE

Then it gives a mobile phone number. Everybody knows the rumour of a medium helping the police, and even your Chief Constable assumed it was me. He was quite happy as long as his crime figure rates dropped. But now he might think it's this bloody woman."

"Calm down, love. Look, even the cat has gone under the sofa. It's obvious it's not her. Anyone that matters knows it's not this woman. She's obviously a fake. Why else would she need to take out a big advert if she was any good?"

"I know I didn't want it to get about that it was me that helped to solve cases, but I don't want this Claire Voyant taking all my glory. The damn cheek of her."

"I tell you what, when I'm at work tomorrow I'll get her file up, if I can find out her real name. I bet she's been done for something and got a record for fraud." He put his arm around her and said, "She couldn't hold a candle next to you, darling. Come on, make me a cuppa and then I'll tell you all about the murder. That always cheers you up."

The Deadly Detective Agency had been conceived in the Becklesfield Public Library, which was where Abigail and her friends met their new clients. Owing to the fact that the whole building had been thought of as haunted for this reason, they changed their posters to say that Deads could only have an appointment for their services after midnight. As it was a Monday morning, the detectives went to Hayley's house for their meeting to see what everyone had found out about Dora's murder.

"How are you today, Hayley?" asked Abigail warily.

"Furious, hun. Did you read about that fake medium? I'm fuming. Not just for me. It's all the people she is conning by saying that she solved your murder and the others. She'll make a fortune and tell them all a pack of lies and whatever they want to hear." Betty and Terry had no idea what they were talking about and were shocked by what they saw in the paper, especially the usually passive Betty.

"Palm readings! Palm readings! I'll give her my palm right round her ruddy chops!" said Betty. "And star charts? She'd be seeing stars, alright!"

"Thank you, hun. That really cheered me up. Tom is going to look into her today. He thinks she's bound to have a record of some kind. I've tried to find a Claire Voyant online, but there's nothing about her. She's just appeared out of nowhere. Honest to God, I could kill the woman. But breathe…" Hayley took some deep breaths and would have meditated if she had the time, but they had a murder to solve, so she gave a brief account of what Tom had told her.

"Betty and I didn't find out much yesterday," said Terry. "Apparently, Dora used to be much more friendly, but whether it was her husband dying or the boys moving away, she changed and lost her spark. She used to be quite stylish as well, but then went all frumpy, so some of my contacts said. And like Betty mentioned, she always wanted to know the ins and outs of a duck's…"

"Ah, I think that will do, thank you, Terry," said Abigail, while nodding towards Suzie. "Well, we had success at the house after the body had been taken away and everyone had gone. First of all, we found another side to our Dora. Hidden in the wardrobe were some sexy undies, a whip, and black PVC gear."

"Well, you're never too old, dear," said Betty. "I remember my John especially used to like it when I…"

"Shall we come back to that later, Betty? Thank you. I might forget a clue if I'm thinking of what you and John got up to," laughed Abigail.

"What was Dora wearing? We might get a time of death if she was in her nightwear," said Terry.

"Good point. We both know all about that, don't we?" Terry

and Abigail both died in bed, so were in their pyjamas for the foreseeable future. "Luckily for her, she wasn't. She had on a grey pleated skirt, cream blouse, and her slippers. You know the type, they were red furry ones with Velcro on the front to get them on and off."

"Ah, now that I do know about," said Betty. "A lady of that age would never wear those if she was expecting a visitor, so I think we can safely say that he or she wasn't invited. And if that was me, if someone had knocked at the door, I would still have taken them off. So, they must have broken in."

"Excellent point, Betty. Now, thanks to Suzie, we found the key to the locked drawer in the writing desk. Can you text Tom later and tell him it's in a needle book in the wicker basket, on top of the fridge? I'm not surprised they didn't find it."

"Will do. Anything else?"

"Also, in that basket was a list of names of people who had donated to the Amber Road Bird Sanctuary. The pub landlord, James Rich, Cassie, the cleaner, and Major Cove. The only name we didn't know was M. Jones."

"I think I can help you there. Mark Jones is one lucky man. He's married to Rebecca Jones," said Terry with a grin. "She's the one with the big…eyes! Very nice lady she is too. Not that I know her. I've only seen her around the village. She's in her twenties, blonde, and gorgeous. I don't know much about him, except that he is the captain of the golf club."

"Hmm, I see. That explains a lot. Tom said he interviewed someone called Rebecca Jones. She was the one who said she saw Dora's argument with the Major. He made out she was in her eighties. I wondered why he went red and looked the other way. I'll make him suffer for that later," Hayley said, smiling. "Oh, and I've just remembered that he found a receipt by her bed for a hotel in Brighton, from roughly eight or nine years ago."

"I think her husband died before then, so I wonder who the

lucky chap was," said Betty. "I bet she took her boots and whip with her."

"Just goes to show that you never really know anyone. Although they say there's more goes on in a village behind the net curtains than anywhere else," said Lillian.

"I know," said Betty. "Did you know that we had a Miss Hussey that used to run a brothel from her house behind the cricket pitch? We had no idea until the police raided it in the seventies. Although now I say it out loud, the name might have been a bit of a clue."

Abigail added, "With all the murders and robberies around here, you make a good point. I'm pretty stumped on this one. And thank you very much, Terry, for your excellent description of Mrs Jones. It's strange that you know how nice she is when you only know her by sight. Not that I care," Abigail said sulkily.

Terry was rather pleased that Abigail sounded rather jealous. Maybe she did care more than she let on. "Put it down to a gut feeling."

"I'm sure it is," she replied and crossed her arms.

"Very funny. Anyway, I'm surprised you haven't worked out who did it yet and why, Abigail," said Terry. He himself was rather jealous of Abigail's brilliance when she solved the crimes and liked to wind her up when she was wrong or didn't have the answers.

"Give her a chance," said Lillian. "It only happened yesterday."

"Weeeell...," said Abigail.

"Oh no," shrieked Terry. "You can't have!"

"Haha. No, of course not. Don't be daft. But I might have worked out a motive. Listen, Dora loved to look at birds, but her binoculars were ready to look out over the green, weren't they, Lillian? Now, as for the newspaper, we thought she was going to cut out an article or an advert about the upcoming pub quiz or something. But we know she refused to go in the Cricketers, so it wasn't that. But what if she was going to cut out letters."

"Like the agony aunt letters, you mean?" asked Betty.

"No, individual letters, like a blackmailer or kidnapper would use. We all know how she liked to hear secrets. She was an expert at finding things out."

"And don't forget the glue we found for sticking them down," said Suzie.

"Brilliant, I had forgotten that. I even know some of her victims."

"No," said Terry. "You mean you can guess some of her victims."

"Well, we know there were at least four of them because she wrote them down on the piece of paper in the basket."

"They gave her money for her bird charity. I told you, she was always volunteering," said Lillian.

"But that was her little joke, you see. Clever Dora, I'm rather impressed. I like that kind of thing. But you're right in a way, those four had donated to The Amber Road Bird Sanctuary."

Hayley nodded and smiled. "Brilliant, hun. Her little joke. It's an anagram - The Dora Bream Bird Sanctuary."

"Precisely," said Abigail and bowed with a flourish.

"Well, my giddy aunt," said Betty. Even Terry was impressed by that. Although Lillian had to explain what it meant to Suzie, who then declared Abigail was marvellous and as good as any of the detectives in the mystery books that she had read in the library.

"So, we have at least four suspects to question at some point, for starters. And Tom said that there's a meeting of the Women's Institute later at the Vicarage. Dora was the chairwoman, so we might learn something about her. There may be others in the village she had her claws into. I know I gave them that talk, but I'm not a member, so I can't go."

"Betty and I could go and eavesdrop," said Lillian. "Unless you want to go, Abigail?"

"Much as I like a good eavesdrop, no, you two go. I have something else in mind."

Betty was so pleased. "I'd love to go and do a bit of earwiggling. I joined after the kids had left home. It was rather good and helped me to fill the hours, and there was always a good cause to help with. I was famous for my strawberry tarts. They'd melt in your mouth. Not for my apricot jam though, unfortunately. I had to throw away my best cast-iron saucepan when my apricot jam set like stone. Even King Arthur would not have been able to pull that wooden spoon out."

"That's hilarious, Betty," laughed Abigail. "Who knows, they may even be still talking about your tarts. Terry, how about you and I go to Dora's, because you haven't seen the scene of the crime yet? Hayley, if you tell Tom about the key, we might be there when they open that bottom drawer."

Terry couldn't tell Abigail how happy he was that they were going to spend some time alone. It was funny, she could drive him crazy, but he missed her when she wasn't there. He was a bachelor, and had never found love while he was alive, and if this was what it was like, he was rather glad. Relationships were more of a mystery than one of their cases!

Chapter 8

IN A BACKSTREET HOTEL IN GOREBRIDGE, misleadingly named The Grand, a husband and wife sat on the hard bed, leaning against a plastic headboard. They had travelled down from London the week before and, even though it was the cheapest place to stay that they could find, money was running out fast. They had booked in under their real names - Hugh and Veronica Stokes, but it was an alias they had invented that they both thought would make them rich. The name Claire Voyant had come to Veronica after her cousin in Gorebridge told her that she had been to a May Day Fayre at a stately home, where a psychic had found a missing boy and even knew where a kidnapped girl was. The girl herself had been giving interviews on the television and in the newspapers, telling anyone who would listen about this marvellous, anonymous medium who had saved her life.

Hugh had been out of prison for less than a year and found it hard to live on just his benefits, and Veronica had no intention of getting a proper job. So, when she came up with this latest con, he was all for it.

"It'll be a piece of cake," she had said. "We'll put an advert in the local paper and wait for the phone to start ringing," she had said. "The only outlay will be the cost of the advert," she had said.

Well, the only phone call they had received so far was from a Mrs Mimms who wanted to know where her dog, Tootles, was. Her husband had left a window open, and the dog had made a run for it. When Claire Voyant had said that she wanted a payment of fifty pounds, Mrs Mimms had replied, "I bet you bloody do!" and rudely cut her off.

So, it was definitely time for a new strategy. "There must be something we can do. Perhaps we need to put something else in the paper. Yes! I've had another brilliant idea, Hugh," said Veronica, jumping up.

"That advert cost more than this hotel does for a night. I say we give it up and go home. We'll try one of the old ones again. The watch one will get us up and running."

Both Hugh and Veronica were good-looking, which helped to swindle their unsuspecting marks. Veronica was an expert at playing the damsel in distress. She would be in tears after having been mugged, and all she had left was a watch that the robbers hadn't seen. Hugh would arrive to tell her saviour that it was worth a lot of money, and he would give her fifty for it. Whether it was greed or chivalry, the punter would give her double that and would be quite happy until he found out that he had paid for a fake that was worth a tenner at most.

Another favourite of Veronica's was when she would pretend to run out of petrol and ask to borrow some money. And then give them her mother's ruby eternity ring as collateral, with a promise to get in touch and give them their money back. Even women would part with thirty pounds for the ring, which was worthless of course. One night they made three hundred pounds. Even when she had run out of rings, she could simply write down their address and promise to send them the money. That only worked on the men though. It was like her superpower. That's why she thought this paranormal lark would be a piece of cake, once she got going.

Other times, it would be Hugh doing a long con, by getting a woman to part with her savings to invest in him. He would show them photos of the beauty spa or gym he was about to open. All he needed was a few thousand more for the equipment, and maybe they could run it together. He usually targeted lonely married women, who couldn't say a word after he disappeared once he had their money. Neither worried if the poor victim happened to be a pensioner or lost every penny they had.

"I'm not giving up, Hugh. I'm bored of all the old ones, and you being in the paper when you got caught and sent down won't help. This will be the best con we've ever done, especially when we get going. Word of mouth will spread it around like wildfire. Anything paranormal is all the rage at the moment. Have you seen how many programmes there are on the telly about ghosts? And when I say we need something else in the newspaper, I don't mean another advert. I mean an actual article about me, about the Great Claire Voyant, so it won't cost a penny. They might even pay us."

"What sort of article? You can't let them have your picture, and it's not like you can tell them how you solved the case of the missing kid, or the other things she's done, is it?"

"That's the beauty of my next idea. You know all these robberies that are happening around here at those big manor houses? There was another one in the paper that happened last week at Cadderly Manor. Well, I'll tell them where they can find the stolen gear from the latest one."

Hugh rolled his eyes. "How the hell are you going to know that, Miss Claire Voyant?"

"Because you are the one that's going to steal it! You did it all the time before we met, and you never got caught. I've got the perfect plan. All you have to do is to break into where that May Day Fayre was held. It's a huge house outside Becklesfield. I think it was called Chiltern Hall."

Chapter 9

MAJOR ROLAND COVE, ROLY TO HIS FRIENDS AT THE golf club, was sitting in his sun chair overlooking his spacious garden. It was his and Esme's pride and joy. They loved doing the pruning and mowing, even the weeding. Normally, his wife would join him for their morning coffee, but since Saturday, he had noticed that she was a bit short with him. Actually, downright nasty at times. When he had told her that he was entering the Becklesfield Trophy next month, she said he could do what he damn well liked. It wasn't like his Esme at all. She had come home in a foul mood that evening and hadn't even cooked his supper. She said she had been to see Mrs Northover, to make sure she had enough bread and milk, and had promptly slammed the lounge door and gone off to bed in a huff.

Maybe it was something called the change he had heard about on the television the other morning. A song came into his head, 'Why can't a woman be more like a man?' and he laughed to himself, thinking of it. He just hoped these moods of hers weren't going to change his life. He'd have to get her some flowers on the way home from lawn bowls tomorrow.

He smiled when he thought about the bit of good news that

he had heard yesterday. Someone had done the village a favour and murdered Dora. He was only surprised that someone hadn't done it years ago. God knows he felt like it himself. There was a time when he was very fond of her, but then things changed and he made sure he kept well away from her. Luckily she never went to the Cricketers so he could treat Esme to a meal from time to time. He even had to stop accompanying her to church on a Sunday because she was always there. But he didn't mind that; it gave him a chance to play a quick round and have a swift drink in the golf clubhouse.

That reminded him, Esme usually had some strong words for him when he got home slightly on the late side, but yesterday she just left his dried-up roast dinner in the oven. She never usually missed the chance to nag him for his tardiness. Yes, it must be the thing that begins with the letter M. Was it men... something. Should begin with women, surely.

"Esme, dear. I've made us coffee. Aren't you going to join me?" he shouted.

No answer. Yes, he had better get her some chocolates as well. Or perhaps take her to see Doctor Chopra to get some tablets for it. The lady on the programme had mentioned something about tablets - HPT or something. That should do the trick. He congratulated himself on his thoughtfulness. He really was a caring husband; Esme was very lucky.

He had left his chair to go and fetch his wife when he heard a car on the gravel at the front of the house, followed by an extremely loud knock. Enough to wake the dead, thought the Major. He was about to give them a piece of his mind when Esme came to the back door and told him he had better come in, as the police had arrived.

Esme offered the visitors a beverage, which they declined, and invited them to sit down. Detective Chief Inspector Johnson took one look at the Major and knew exactly the type he was. Moreover, it was the type he hated. He had one of those stupid cravats on for a start, and Johnson would bet a fiver that somewhere he had a tweed jacket with those leather patches on the elbows. As if he needed to have his stuff patched. Unlike when he was a boy, and his mum had sewed any material she could find on the knees of his trousers.

Sergeant Mills took out his notebook and Johnson leaned forward to start with his questions. "We have witnesses, Mrs. Cove, that you were seen going into Dora Bream's house shortly before she was brutally murdered. Can you tell me what you were doing there?"

"Well, I wasn't murdering her, Inspector."

"It is Detective Chief Inspector."

"Nevertheless, I received a call from her on Friday evening asking me to pop in and see her after she had done the church flowers on Saturday. As I had a lot on that day, I didn't get there until roughly six-thirty."

"And what did she want you to go for?"

"Nothing out of the ordinary. She was due to chair the WI committee meeting this afternoon in the Vicarage, and she wanted me to tell her what funds we had available for different upcoming events. I'm the treasurer, you see."

"So what time did you leave?"

"I only stayed for about half an hour, if that. So maybe seven o'clock."

"Did she make you tea, Mrs. Cove?"

"No."

"I find that hard to believe, because you lot are always big on etiquette. That is unless…."

"Unless I was going to strangle her to death?"

"How do you know that was the cause of death?"

The Major couldn't stay quiet any longer. "Really, Detective, is this really necessary? In this village, if you sneeze, someone will know, so with something as juicy as a murder, this end of the village will hear all about it before the police can answer the phone."

"We'll get to you in a minute, Mr. Cove," snapped Johnson.

"Major, if you don't mind," he snapped back.

Mills could sense an altercation coming and so asked a question of his own.

"Mrs Cove, she asked you to give her the figures as the treasurer, but I can't remember any of the witnesses mentioning you were carrying a briefcase or a folder. Can you explain that?"

"It wasn't an official meeting, and I carry most of that information in my head. This afternoon, for instance, I will be taking all the documents and statements with me, in my briefcase."

"Will it still go ahead even after the murder?" asked a surprised Mills.

"Of course, Sergeant. The Women's Institute didn't stop for war and it definitely won't stop for a death."

Johnson turned to look at the Major with glee in his eye. "So where were you on Saturday evening, Sir?" This startled the Major. He was still taking in that Esme had lied to him when she had said she was visiting old Mrs Northover about her shopping. She never mentioned popping in to see Dora.

"Sorry? Me? I had been at the Cricketers Inn at lunchtime and I got back here about fourish. Then I sat in this very chair and watched a bit of sport. The Scottish Open was on, golf, you know. If I remember correctly, I fell asleep for a while, then carried on watching it until the coverage had finished. I'm sure you can find out what time that was. In fact, I can confirm my wife was telling the truth about the time she arrived home. And then I pootled around here doing something or other. I didn't go out again until I had a round of golf the next day."

"So you can verify that your husband was here all night, Mrs. Cove?"

"Hmm, I can, although I had an awful headache when I got back and went upstairs to lie down. But I'm sure he was here if that's what he's claiming," she said and narrowed her eyes as she gave her husband an evil look. "He got in bed around midnight, so he was definitely here from then onwards."

"But, but of course, I was here, Esme. You must have heard the television and me moving about."

"The sound of the television is not an alibi, Sir."

"But why would I have wanted to kill poor Dora?" said the Major, while getting increasingly flustered.

"You tell me, Sir," said Johnson. "Maybe it had to do with the argument you were seen having on the High Street last week. Quite a heated one by all accounts. We have witnesses that say you grabbed her by the arm at one point."

"Absolute piffle. She had made a mountain out of a molehill, as usual. I had only said... what was it now? Er, I know, I said she would have to move the final of the bowls competition because it clashed with a golf tournament I'm organising. That's right. And she got most annoyed with me. As I'm sure you will find out, Mrs Bream liked to run this village all by herself, didn't she, Esme? She'll tell you."

"That's very true, but I'm surprised that she would care about lawn bowls, as she never played," his wife said maliciously. "Now, if it had been a bridge tournament, I would have agreed."

Johnson played an ace of his own. He was going to enjoy this. "So it wasn't anything to do with threatening to tell everyone that you spent a night in the Royal Hotel in Brighton with her?"

The Major went pale, and even Mills was surprised that Johnson had brought that up in front of his wife. That was cruel, not that he had any sympathy for him, but he did for the poor lady. Although she didn't look particularly shocked, more annoyed.

"That is totally untrue. How dare you suggest that. I'll have you for slander. I play golf with your Chief Constable, and I will inform him as soon as…"

"I will stop you there, Sir. We have the exact date you stayed there several years ago. Unfortunately for you, she kept the receipt as a souvenir. We rang the hotel this morning, and they confirmed that you were both there together, and paid by a debit card from your personal account." The Major's shoulders visibly sagged. "Did you know about this, Mrs Cove?"

"Of course not. I would never have put up with that. I own Grey Towers. This was my family home long before we got married, and believe me, I would have given my husband his marching orders, and thrown his golf clubs out the door after him."

"Do you know what I think, Mrs Cove? I think she told you about the sordid little affair on Saturday and that's why she invited you round there, because your husband had broken it off, and she wanted to pay him back. You've both got a motive."

The Major got to his feet. "But that's not true. That night in Brighton was the last night we spent together. I broke it off way back then. I promise, Esme. Why would she wait nearly ten years?"

"I don't know yet, but I'll find out," said Johnson, as his phone rang and he answered it without getting up.

"Johnson… Yes, I see… Is that right?… Very useful… Ta very much." He gave a broad smile, which was in itself unusual, and told the Major to sit back down. "The autopsy has just been done. You'll enjoy this, Mills. And you, Mrs Cove. It would seem that the silk scarf that was used to throttle the old dear wasn't a scarf at all. It was, in actual fact, a cravat, just like the one you are wearing. Get the uniforms to start a search, Sergeant. And I think you had better come to the station with us, Major Cove."

Chapter 10

POLICE CONSTABLE TOM BENNETT HAD SPENT THE last hour walking along Becklesfield High Street, asking if anyone had either seen Dora Bream late on Saturday, or had seen the argument that had taken place with Major Cove on the Wednesday. Plenty had seen her leaving the church and buying a few things in the village shop, but only Mrs Merry, from the flower shop, had seen them shouting at each other. But as hard as she had tried, she couldn't hear what was being said.

Tom then tried the charity shop – 'Wet & Wildlife'. He knew this was Hayley's favourite shop. She would have a clear-out and take a bagful to donate, but then would come home with two bags. Skirts mainly, or any unusual ornaments, which she would then take back the next time.

Hang on a minute, he thought, and stopped in his tracks. Surely not. That's what he had got Hayley for her birthday last year! He'd gone to a lot of trouble to find that after he saw the advert. It was the latest thing, a 'Musical Magic Masseur'. You put it over your shoulders, and it rippled. Not only that, it played three different tunes in violin, cello, or accordion. How ungrateful. He knew she loved all that reiki stuff and thought it would be the perfect present. And for goodness sake, was that the yellow coat he'd bought her for Christmas? And hang on a minute, surely they were his tartan trousers that he'd got himself when he was thinking of taking up golf! A tall, middle-aged gentleman came from the back of the shop, stopping him from checking if any more of his things were for sale. Harry Harding was the manager and said he knew Dora Bream rather well.

"She volunteered here, but not on a regular basis. She just filled in when someone was off or we were short-staffed. I think she did a morning a few weeks ago, a Thursday, if I remember rightly. It was just me and her, and she sorted the donations out in the back and then went on the till if anyone bought something."

"Did anything out of the ordinary happen? Or did she say she was in trouble or worried about anything?"

"Quite the opposite. She seemed very cheerful and chatted with most of the customers. I asked her if she had come into money, as she was so cheerful. She even gave me a donation herself, which she never had done before."

"Why was that unusual? I know she liked birds."

"Yes, she liked birds, but here we collect mainly for foxes and badgers, among other things, and I know for a fact she'd hired someone to kill the fox that kept going into her garden. And she was all for culling badgers. She said they kept digging holes in her lawn. And don't get her started on squirrels! They ate the nuts that she put out for her birds. I asked her once why she wanted to work here, and she said she did it to support the village and because she wanted to meet people. A very mixed personality was our Dora."

"I thought that myself, Sir. I can't get a handle on her at all."

"I was grateful for her help, but I can't say I liked her. There was something about her that I can't put my finger on. But don't go thinking that I'd want to kill her. I'm about saving lives, and I have no wish to spend the rest of my life in jail over her, I can assure you."

"It never crossed my mind, Sir. I don't suppose you can remember who came in that day, can you, Mr Harding?"

"I could look at the receipts of those that paid by card, but most pay by cash around here. And as you can see, I haven't got time to look. I'm on my own today. But we really need the donations, so I can't just close the shop. Those poor little badgers and bees…" he said, raising his eyebrows.

"Ah, I see. I don't think we need you to tell us who came in for now," he said, while checking his pockets for cash. Unfortunately, he could only find a crisp, new note. Although, he was tempted to say that from the looks of it, he had already given enough, so forget it.

"Thank you very much, Constable. The wildlife of the River Gore and Ridgeway Woods are very grateful."

They better be, thought Tom. That was for his lunch! He went two doors down, into the Post Office, as the fight had taken place near there. He asked Miss Spittle if she had seen or heard anything, but she hadn't and didn't think that Dora had come in at all on Wednesday, as that was the day she went to the library. And that was like clockwork. So, he went to the shop next door which was Banning's Antiques.

He needed to talk to the owner anyway as he was seen walking past Dora's house. That made him think of Rebecca as she had been the one to see him. Tom thought he had handled it very well and Hayley didn't suspect anything. He told her that Mills and he had only got anything helpful from the old ladies that lived up that end of the village. It was a Mrs Northover and, ooh, who was it now? Umm, he thought her name was Mrs Jones. She hadn't even noticed. Not that anything had happened, but he still felt a bit guilty for some reason.

He pushed open the door to the sound of a bell tinkling over his head and carefully went down the worn step into the antique shop, which was old in its own right. Julian Banning was a tall, thin, slightly balding man in his forties, wearing a beige cardigan with leather buttons, that Johnson would have hated, thought Tom. He would think of that as a sign of the upper class, but in a place like Becklesfield, it was almost a uniform. As the owner was talking to a young, good-looking lad with curly hair, he took the time to look around.

Tom had the feeling that he couldn't get any more stock in there if he had tried. Every wall was full with paintings, brass ornaments, and weapons from different centuries. Dark, wooden furniture gave the shop a dismal feel and Tom noticed there wasn't a price sticker on any of it. A sure sign that Hayley and he wouldn't be able to afford anything. Not that it would have looked right in their house. Hayley was all about lightness and space. He saw a spooky, porcelain Victorian doll and could imagine what she would say about that. She'd take one look and say it was possessed by an old woman, more likely than not. Life was never dull with his mystic wife. But on the counter, where the till was situated, he saw some jewellery in a glass case. Now, that was the kind of thing that Hayley would love. It was her birthday in about a month and he'd better try a bit harder this time, or he might as well give it straight to the charity shop. Wives were so hard to buy for.

Julian Banning was not surprised to see a uniformed policeman in his shop. Dora's murder had been the talk of the village, and the publicity might even bring some buyers into the high street. The curly-haired young man ignored Tom and walked out the door.

"I suppose someone told you that I was near the scene of the crime, Constable. I walk past there most nights. But I can't say for sure as I haven't a clue when the murder took place."

"We've not narrowed that down yet, Sir. Sometime Saturday evening, we think. The post-mortem is being done this morning, so we'll know more then. It was mentioned that you were seen close to her house around sevenish. Did you see anyone going in or out, or behaving suspiciously?"

"Hmm, I'll try, but that was two days ago. I think I saw Esme Cove closing the gate as if she had been inside, and the way that she slammed it, I would say it wasn't a pleasant visit. But I'm pretty sure that it was that house. I was a bit tired by that point. But I definitely saw Rebecca Jones though. She waved at me through her front window. You can't forget seeing our Becks. Have you had the pleasure, yourself?"

"I've questioned her if that's what you mean, Mr Banning?" Tom answered defensively. "Were you on your way home at that point?"

"Yes, I was. I was a bit later than usual as I'd had a late customer who wanted me to look at some family heirlooms and give him a price. So, I went home and crashed on the sofa with a microwave meal and a well-earned beer. No alibi, alas, as I live on my own. But I can assure you that I would have no reason to kill an old woman. I hardly knew her. I can't remember ever seeing her in the Greyhound or the Cricketers, where I spend a lot of my time. And I don't go to church unless it's a wedding or a funeral. Different worlds, you see? Is it right that she was strangled?"

"I can't say yet, Sir. Not until there's an official cause of death. Did you witness an argument last week between her and Major Cove?"

"An argument between those two wasn't that rare. I saw them on the village green a while ago, and they didn't look that friendly. I did see the one last week, as a matter of fact. I couldn't miss it. It got quite heated and was right outside the shop."

"Did you hear what was said?"

"I'm not a nosy gossip like some round here, you know? But as it happened," he said with a smile, "I had to move something in the window and I heard her say something like it was time it all came out once and for all. But I've no idea what. Then he made a grab for her, and she pushed him and stormed off."

"Had she or the Major been in here?"

"Before the row, you mean? Er, I don't think so. Not that I can remember." Tom thought he could be lying.

"If you do remember she had, I'd appreciate you letting me or one of the detectives know. Who was the young man that was just here? Does he work for you?"

"That was Chris, the local odd job man. He helps out when I need something moved or delivered. He drives the van. As you can see, some of these pieces weigh a ton."

"You've got some nice stuff here, Mr Banning. I might come back here with my wife. She's got a birthday coming up, and it might be better if she chose something herself this time. She'd love these bracelets; they're so unusual. Are they very old?"

"Not especially, but they are very rare. The quality of the jade on this one is remarkable."

"How much would it cost?" Tom asked.

"I could let you have it for three hundred."

"Mmm. A bit out of a constable's price range." He saw a black and gold ornate brooch and knew that was what he wanted to get for Hayley. "What about that brooch at the back?"

Julian Banning lifted it out carefully.

"You have good taste. It's gold and enamel and is what's called mourning jewellery. Very collectable and a good example of Victorian craftsmanship."

"Morning, as in the ladies wore it in the mornings?" he asked.

"No, Sergeant." He lifted a catch and opened the brooch to show Tom the hidden compartment. "Mourning as in the deceased. That is a lock of someone's hair. Sometimes it was just a photograph, especially if it was a locket. The Victorians knew how to remember their loved ones. In the basket over there are photographs of dead family members, propped up and dressed in their Sunday best."

"You're kidding. Someone's dead relative's hair. Hmm. How much is the brooch, not that my wife is getting it? I think I'll stick to her perfume."

"The gold is eighteen carat, so that would set you back about eight hundred and fifty pounds." Even if he could afford it, he could just imagine the ghosts that could suddenly appear to Hayley. The last thing he wanted was a Victorian man or child running amok in his house. He had enough trouble with the ones he had now.

Tom was quite happy to hear his phone ring. "I'm sorry, Sir, I have to take this. But that's all for now. Someone might need to speak to you again." He left the shop to the sound of the tinkling bell and said hello to his wife. "Hi, love. I was just thinking of you. I was in the antique shop getting ideas for your birthday present."

"As long as you don't get me one of those creepy, old china dolls."

"You must be psychic; I was looking at one, but I know better than that. Is it anything important? I'm in the high street trying to find any witnesses to that row."

"It is quite, hun. The key for the desk drawer that you were after, I have a reliable source that says it's in the kitchen, in a needle book, in a wicker basket."

"That is helpful. I think I can guess who told you. I looked in there myself and never saw it. I'll have to cancel the locksmith if he hasn't been. Anything else you can share?"

"Abi reckons that Dora could be a blackmailer." Hayley went on to explain the reasons why.

"That makes a lot of sense. Perhaps there's something in that locked drawer."

"I'm outside the library; I want to talk with the librarian. Apparently, Dora used to go in there a lot."

"Be careful. It's alright for the others; they can't get hurt for snooping. Got to go, sweetheart, there's another call. It's Mills. Talk later."

Tom couldn't quite believe that Johnson had made an arrest already. And he was so enjoying being part of a murder investigation again. He told Mills that he had a sudden idea of where the missing key might be and said as soon as he had checked it out, he would go to Grey Towers and help the other uniforms to search the premises. With a feeling of disappointment, he walked slowly back to the scene of the crime once more.

Hayley took a slow walk around looking at the books. She needed to have something to have a chance to talk to the librarian. Rather than get a paranormal or self-help book like she usually did, she picked up a book about owning a cat. Although, she rather thought that Luna owned them. The little kitten only had to purr and she was fed, jump on them in the morning and they had to get up, and he slept when he chose to and not the other way round. Hayley and Tom never expected to have a cat. She'd always had dogs when she was young, but now they both loved him like their baby. The book called '101 Things a Cat Expects of You', would help.

Hayley went to the counter to check out her book, hoping Janette would be friendly after what she'd noticed her doing in the past, like talking to herself.

"Oh, are you a cat person?" she asked and actually smiled at her.

"Yes, I suppose I am now. I found a near-dead kitten and nursed it back to health. He's a beautiful tortoiseshell. We love him to bits. What about you? Have you got one, Janette, isn't it?"

"I did have one. She was ginger, with lovely markings. She went missing a few months ago. I'm always looking out for her. I called her Tilly. I still put her food out in the garden every morning and call her every night. It makes it harder not knowing if she has crossed the rainbow bridge. I'd much rather know one way or the other. I might even get another cat. I could kick myself for not putting a collar on her. I took it off because she'd got it caught on a branch the day before. I'd had her for five years and she'd always had it on. I blame myself."

"You know what cats are like; she might be getting fed from another house."

"Not Tilly. She was a mummy's girl. Once she was back in the house, she never left my side. If I went in the kitchen then she did. It's like losing a member of the family."

"She might suddenly turn up one day. I'll say a prayer for her. I don't know what I'd do if Luna ran off. I think I'll just keep him as an indoor one. He's too young to go out yet anyway. It's a dangerous world out there. Did you hear about Dora? I can't believe it, can you? I used to see her at church."

"I was just saying to my friend, Harry, that she used to come in here every Wednesday. She'd get two racy novels at a time. She'd never say more than thank you. I think she was a bit embarrassed about them. The image of a church-going philanthropist did not exactly go with 'Stripping for Victory'," giggled Janette.

"I'll say," laughed Hayley. "I would never have guessed. Well, I suppose she had been a widow and been on her own for a long time, so why not?"

"Well, I'm not too sure she was. But that's just gossip, so I'm not saying a word more. Here's your book," said Janette, putting an end to the conversation.

"Thank you very much. And I'm so sorry to hear about Tilly. Nice talking to you, Janette."

"You too, Mrs Bennett. Enjoy the cat book."

Hayley left with it under her arm, as the truth slowly dawned on her, and she wasn't sure whether to laugh or cry.

Tom felt a cold column of air as he looked in the kitchen for the key. He had a feeling he wasn't alone and shivered. "Hello,

Abigail or Betty or whoever. I know you're trying to help, but please can you not do anything to scare me."

Unbeknown to Tom, Abigail put her hands on her hips. "That's charming, isn't it, Terry? After all we do. Mind you, I can't blame him."

"At least we can see what's in the drawer now. I'm hoping it's a list of her blackmail victims with a big X next to the killer's name."

"We should be so lucky," said Abigail. They weren't so lucky. In fact, the only thing in there was a folder with her bank statements. Also, a padded box containing a ring, with a receipt for the antique gold, bloodstone, shield signet ring, which Tom bagged and took away with him.

Once he got safely to the door, he turned back and said, "In case there are any spirits here, Roland Cove has been arrested, so we won't be needing the help of The Deadly Detective Agency, thank you very much."

Chapter 11

BACK AT HAYLEY'S HOUSE, A VERY FRUSTRATED Abigail sat in the conservatory. Tiggy was settled on her lap, and Luna, the kitten, was curled up on Hayley's. "All I'm saying is, if Johnson has arrested Major Cove, he's got to be innocent."

"Never mind about the murder for a minute, I've got something really important to tell you," said Hayley.

"Now you've got me worried, what is it?"

"It's rather sad, actually. I went to ask Janette in the library about Dora, who incidentally didn't know much about her, apart from the fact that she might not have been the lonesome widow. So that fits in with what Tom told us. But listen to this, we got talking about cats, and this shocked me to the core. She said she had a ginger cat with lovely markings that had disappeared a few months ago and she couldn't get over it and still looked everywhere for her." They both looked down at the ginger cat that was purring loudly on Abigail's lap.

"You mean Tiggy is actually her cat that died. But she thinks she is just missing. Oh no. The poor woman. Of course, there's no way Tiggy could tell us, although I did see her following

Janette around at times, but never took any notice. You poor little kitty cat, you couldn't tell us."

"It's awful, hun. She opens the back door for her every night in case she comes back. And in the morning, she puts a bowl of food outside the back door. Honestly, Abi, I could weep. And the funny thing is that she was called Tilly. I mean, how strange is that? Tilly is now Tiggy. If that's not kismet, I don't know what is. She can't have had any idea that she was pregnant. No wonder Tiggy feels right at home and comes when we call her."

"That's thanks to Suzie, because of her tiger markings. I'd named her Carrot. What can we do?"

"I'll go and talk to her. I'll have to. She needs to know. In fact, I have a very good idea. Leave it with me." Hayley picked up Luna and gave him a kiss on his nose.

"So, Janette is your nanny. Don't worry, we'll look after her for you, sweetie. Now we'd better get back to the murder. Where were we?"

"I was just saying if Johnson has arrested Roland, then he must be innocent," said Abigail emphatically.

"Not necessarily, hun. If you put it all together, it is quite damning." Hayley counted the reasons on her fingers. "One - she was strangled with a cravat. There are photos of him wearing that exact one when he won the mixed doubles at bowls last year. Two - he admitted to having an affair with Dora. Three - she threatened to tell his wife and probably did by the sound of it. Four - and going by the bank statements, Tom is sure he was being blackmailed by her."

"Yeah, but apart from that... But look, someone could be setting him up. And didn't Tom say that he was burgled not long ago? Perhaps he or she stole the cravat then. It might have even been the wife, Esme. No doubt she would have loved to set him up for murder. We only have her word that she found out about the fling on Saturday afternoon. Dora could have told her over the phone and then she went round with the cravat. She had just as many reasons to kill her as he did. Mind you, if that was me, I would've killed him."

"Me too. Talking of back-stabbers, Tom couldn't find anything about that Claire Voyant. Let's hope she's gone back to where she came from. Although I couldn't sleep last night for worrying about it. I have an awful feeling that it's not over and I see a sword above my head and a dark cloud in my future thanks to her."

"Don't worry, Hayl, it's just another job for us detectives. There's only one Hayley Moon. Leave it with me. I protect my friends to the death, although most of them are, so don't worry. If she's dodgy, I'll find out and expose her, for sure. I wonder how Lillian and Betty are getting on at the committee meeting. Where did Terry go?"

"He asked Suzie to look at some headstones in the graveyard with him. Any idea why?"

"Do you remember when we did that stakeout? He was sure that he had been at that old house before because he knew things before we even got inside. He described the fireplace and other things. No way could he have known half the things that he was saying. Yet he thought he had been in that orphanage since he was born. He knew they were farmers' tied cottages, and I think he had actually lived there, probably until he was five or six. So we've been trying to find out why no one ever told him. I didn't want to get his hopes up, but he could even have had brothers and sisters out there. He's been dead a long time, but there could still be nieces and nephews around. He spent his whole life thinking he was alone in the world. He never married either, bless him. I said we could look in the library for any census that was done in the thirties, but with all the cases we've taken on lately, we haven't got round to it. We thought that's one way of doing it, or the church keeps records somewhere as well, don't they?"

"They do. I think Pete would be able to help there. There's

an old church Bible and a register where they used to write all the births and deaths of the parishioners in. I'm sure it's in the actual church somewhere, probably in the vestry. I'll make up some story and get him to show me. I'm sure he wouldn't mind. How amazing if we could find a family for Terry. Maybe that will make him want to pass over."

Abigail hoped not; she didn't want him going anywhere. "Can I tell you something, Hayl? And promise that you won't tell the others."

"Of course I won't. You know me better than that, I hope."

"Yeah, sorry. It's just that I'm getting, well, feelings for Terry. I know it's stupid. Especially when half the time he's rude to me. I obviously drive him up the wall, and most of the time he does me. What do you think? It's funny, he's so not my type. But my types haven't got me far before."

"I think it's wonderful, hun. He's definitely got feelings for you, trust me."

"What kind of feelings though? Revulsion perhaps?" she said jokingly.

"No, nothing like that. Do you know, that makes a lot of sense. All the times he's had a go at you might just be because he can't tell you how he really feels. I'm sure he likes you as well."

"He's got a funny way of showing it. Remember when he said I was bossy, domineering, bigheaded…"

"Well, I'm not saying it's an exact science," she laughed.

"So you're saying he's horrible to me because he likes me. Hmm, no wonder I was single. Love is so complicated. But I tell you what, if he ever decided to move on, I think I would be devastated. How crazy is that?"

"Not crazy, hun. Surprising, but not crazy. I tell you what, I bet you a hundred pounds that he's falling for you too."

"Oh my, imagine how horrible he's going to be if he fell in love with me!"

Hayley put her finger to her lips and told Abigail to be quiet. "What's the matter?"

"I heard something, hun. A woman's voice calling my name. It's very faint, and I heard it last night and it woke me up. I assumed it was just a dream, but I don't think so now. It sounded desperate."

"You do have to go through a lot. I can't see anyone here, Hayl. Can you still hear it?"

"Not at the moment, but I will, I suspect. I'm getting the letter L. Maybe the name Lou. It's definitely someone that needs me to help them. It's not Dora, I do know that. Could be something small, like a message. But there's a cry in her voice that has got me worried. When you see Terry, can you ask him to keep an eye out for a lady who might have recently arrived? It could simply be that she's passed and doesn't know what's happened. But if I'm truthful, Abigail, I've got a really bad feeling about this. This lady is hurting. This lady is in trouble. I can't even say if this lady is alive or dead."

"Let me know if I can do anything."

"Just keep a lookout for her, please. Now I've got an errand to run. I'll tell you all about it, if I can get what I'm after."

Terry himself was at that moment wading through the long grass on the far edge of the churchyard. "Where exactly are we going?" asked Suzie.

"I've checked all the main headstones and there's no sign of anyone with my name. Mind you, some of them are covered in moss or worn away. Yet I'm sure I used to live here at some point before I was in the orphanage. How else would I have known that house? I'm thinking maybe my dad was a farmer, as they were tied cottages at one time, so were we so poor that my mum and dad's family couldn't afford a proper burial? Over in this corner are the paupers' graves that are only marked by hand-made wooden crosses, if anything. But if I'm lucky someone might have carved at least their names somewhere. So

I would really appreciate it if you could move any grass or leaves out of the way and look for me. The name we're looking for is anyone Styles. I have no idea of their first names."

"I would love to help you, Terry. Sometimes the others think I'm too young to be involved with some of the cases, but although I was nine when I died, I'm older than that in so many ways."

"I'll make sure the others know that, I promise. Now, what is this one?" There was a stick standing upright amongst the weeds, but if it marked the remains of someone, it was long forgotten. They found pieces of wood and large stones marking the place of burials and were just going to give up when they saw two crosses on their sides against the wall. Suzie brushed away the long grass and years of foliage that had fallen on them. Someone had taken care to mark their resting place. Two branches had been tied together with twine to form a cross. The string crumbled as Suzie lifted it to read the carving on it.

"I can't read it all, but it looks like J something something K then ST something LES. This is it, Terry. Jack Styles. There's no date but this has to be it, doesn't it?"

"It's got to be, I reckon. That or a grandparent, but I've a feeling it's my father for some reason. I can't thank you enough. Could you look at the other one for me?"

"There's not much left. But I think it says Teresa, then an S. It's your mum, I think. Teresa S. Does that mean anything to you, Terry?"

"I really wish it did. But at least we have proper names to look up now. We can maybe find the marriage certificate or something."

"I could do that for you as well. And then we can see if they had a child called Terry. This is one of the most exciting cases we've worked on. My family were everything to me; that's why I still visit my mum and brother. I'd love you to find some family."

"Don't forget they would be over a hundred now, silly."

"I know that. But you never know. We could work out your family tree and find a whole lot of little Styles. Somebody made those crosses with care and loved them enough to scratch their names on them. Let's go back and tell the others."

Chapter 12

THE HOUSE WAS DEATHLY QUIET WITHOUT HER, AND it had somehow got dark and he hadn't noticed, and Lucy hated the dark. They always had to sleep with the landing light on. Matthew Rider was really panicking now. He had rung the police, but they were no help whatsoever. He couldn't make them understand just how worried he was. They said there was nothing they could do. They didn't realise it wasn't like his Luce to go off. It was almost like they were humouring him, and insinuating she had met another man. He would try ringing her best friend, Penny, in a minute. They had been friends since their school days, so if she did have a boyfriend, they would have talked about it. He knew in his heart that wouldn't be it. She loved her home and her comforts. She loved him.

But he had a feeling that something had happened to her on her way back from work on Friday. He really should be at work himself, but luckily for him, he had no one to answer to. His customers would just have to wait a while longer. In fact, they could do their own bloody taxes for a change. He wouldn't be able to concentrate on invoices and the like. He was always home before Lucy. She usually caught the five thirty-five bus and got back about six, by the time it had been round all the villages. He'd seen a lot of police cars going through Becklesfield lately. He wondered if they had found Lucy's body at first, but nobody called to tell him, so something else must have happened by the village green. The desk sergeant he spoke to on the phone did say that they were busy and they would get someone to phone him, but that was yesterday.

Matthew wondered if he should get in the car and drive into Gorebridge. But where would he look? No, he'd stay here in case she phoned or came back. There was a time he could have gone and asked the neighbours if they knew anything. But their friends on either side had both moved. On the left, there was a family with two children under five, so they didn't have much in common with them. And the house to the right was now owned by a chap who lived on his own. Matthew had thought him a bit on the strange side. He kept to himself and didn't even say morning if he walked past. Their old neighbours had invited them round for barbecues on a weekend and drinks at Christmas, but these never even bothered.

He rang some more people, but no one knew a thing. Penny's phone didn't even ring. She must be away or she had changed her number. It was black as pitch now, and he hated to think that she might be out there somewhere, hurt or scared for a second night.

"Where are you, Lucy?" he said again. "Please come home."

Chapter 13

DETECTIVE CHIEF INSPECTOR JOHNSON HAD BEEN bullying Roland Cove and his solicitor for two hours, after a night in the cells. Sergeant Mills thought that he needed a break, let alone the suspect.

"Let's start again, Mr Cove, do you own a cravat, made by Boyes & Son? I am showing the accused a cravat, dark red with fancy gold patterns on it."

Roland shook his head and sighed. "Fleur-de-lis symbols."

"Oh, sorry. Fleur-de-lis," Johnson said sarcastically. "Thank you for illuminating us commoners on that, Sir. I'll be sure to call them that at your trial to the judge. And I'll get some embroidered on your prison uniform when they lock you up for murder. But if you would be so good as to tell us, is this your cravat?"

"Yes. I've already said I own one like it. I have no idea how it ended up at Dora's. As I said, our house was burgled about a week ago, and I thought at the time there wasn't much stolen. Just some of Esme's costume jewellery and a bottle of my best single malt whisky, but nothing of value whatsoever. Of course, I didn't notice a cravat had gone. I have quite a few of them. The police even came out. Check if you don't believe me. It's obvious someone is trying to frame me for Dora's murder."

"Anyone can smash a window and say they've been robbed. For the tape, I'm showing Roland Cove a photograph of Dora Bream's body. You can see your cravat wrapped tightly around the poor lady's neck. Did she let you in, or did you simply walk in the garden door?"

"I told you, I haven't been there for ages. Did you find any of my fingerprints?"

"I think you'd be clever enough to not leave any."

"But stupid enough to kill her with my own cravat."

"Well, you said it, Sir. Maybe it wasn't premeditated, but she pushed you too far this time."

Sergeant Mills pulled the photograph of the crime scene towards himself and squinted. To the right of the body was a shaft of light. Anyone else would have thought it was a ray of sunshine coming in through the window. And was that an orb next to it? Mills wondered if perhaps the rumours were true. He might mention it to Tom if he had the chance.

But Johnson had moved on. "Right then, let's look at motives. According to the villagers, Dora was a popular member of the church and did a lot for charity. So apart from you and your wife, no one has a motive. Perhaps you think Mrs Cove did it then."

"Well, it wasn't me. But of course, I don't think it's Esme. But then again, who knows? She did fail to tell me she had gone to her house that night. She made out she had gone to visit Mrs Northover."

"So let's go back to your affair with Dora. You say it finished years ago, but we only have your word for that."

"It's the truth. Dora's husband had died at last and she wanted me to leave Esme. She was different in those days. I hadn't long left the army and I was bored and fed up. She was full of life back then and fulfilled me in many ways. I don't think it was ever love." Johnson pulled a face at the thought. "But I wouldn't leave Esme for her, as she had the money from her inheritance and Grey Towers was in her name. All I had was my military pension, so I said no. And looking back, I realised I loved my Esme. Dora never forgave me for that, not that I can blame her. I behaved appallingly. She wasn't prepared to be the other woman, so we had a last night in a five-star hotel on the coast, and that's when I told her that it was over. I'm not being big-headed, but she was never the same again. The light went out of her, and any love she had was turned to hate for me and the whole world. Even her appearance changed. I think she gave up trying. That is all there is to say on the matter. I definitely wouldn't kill her because I already felt guilty for ruining her life, Detective."

"Tell us about the argument you were seen having with Dora in the High Street last week."

"Yes, well, she said she wanted to talk to me about something. I obviously thought she meant about her telling Esme, so I did shout at her, but looking back, I think it was something else. I've no idea what."

"We found a very expensive men's signet ring in her desk that she had bought in Banning's Antiques. Are you sure that she wasn't trying to get back with you?"

Major Cove laughed. "Absolutely not. That ship had sailed. Perhaps she had found someone else then. I have no idea."

"I see. So when did she start blackmailing you?" said Johnson with a grin. The major and his solicitor both protested at the sudden change of subject.

"She was doing no such thing," shouted Roland Cove.

"Do you have any proof of my client being blackmailed?" asked the solicitor.

"We have statements from both parties showing his private account being drained and Dora Bream's increasing weekly. She had been depositing large amounts of cash in The Home Counties National Bank for the last five years, as the same amount left yours. She was a very wealthy woman when she died. Whereas your bank is eight hundred pounds overdrawn. Is that why you decided she had to die?"

He shrugged his shoulders. "I spend a lot of money. I don't deny that. I'm a member of the golf club, among other things, and I like to entertain. I'm sure if she was blackmailing people, there are others she had a lot more on than me. Could be anyone. I know for a fact that Reverend Stevens couldn't stand her, but she was always at the church and she moved to the top of the Women's Institute very quickly. Lady Cummings used to be in charge. And she couldn't stand James, the landlord of the Cricketers, so I don't know what had gone on there. Then there's Mark Jones, the captain of Becklesfield Golf Club. He actually said he could kill her one day. I could go on."

"I think you will have to release my client, don't you? It could be any number of people."

Johnson was saving the best for last. "But we didn't find the victim's brown bag and purse outside their house, in a rubbish bin, did we?"

Chapter 14

THE ENTIRE DEADLY DETECTIVE AGENCY, APART FROM Hayley, were sitting on their usual chairs in the Becklesfield Public Library, which had closed for the night. It was quiet and that was better for them, but it meant that Hayley couldn't join them, unless she wanted to be done for breaking and entering.

Lillian, Betty, and Abigail were amazed to hear that Terry had at last found out the names of his parents. Suzie had been on the computer but could find no sign of a Jack and Teresa Styles' marriage certificate. They wondered if they had come to Becklesfield for work and without knowing where they were from, it was going to be hard to find anything about them. The only hope of finding out if they had had a child called Terry was through the church records. For that, they would need Hayley's help. Terry had never seen his birth certificate and never had the need to get one.

Lillian and Betty were waiting to tell the others what they had found out at the Women's Institute meeting.

"The main thing we noticed," said Lillian, "was that no one seemed at all sad that Dora had been murdered. Sir Edward Cummings' wife, Fiona, chaired the meeting for the first time in a while and seemed very happy about it. The other ladies congratulated her on getting the chair back. Dora must have had a hold over her, so we need to add her to the list. She started the meeting by saying how sorry she was that one of their members had died, and asked if anyone would like to say anything on Dora's behalf, but no one did. So she changed the subject and started talking about next month's whist drive."

Betty added, "I feel a bit sorry for her if she had no friends. No wonder she turned bitter. I think the major was the one person she loved and when he ended things it was the end of her world. I know my John drove me up the wall, but we did love each other. And when one of the ladies said that she'd had to have her Labrador put to sleep, they were all most upset. A lot more than they were about Dora. It goes without saying that Esme wasn't there. She's another victim in this. If her husband is convicted of murder, she won't want to show her face again. All Fiona said about her absence was that they would get the budget report at the next meeting. The major wasn't mentioned at all. Then Mary came in with the tea trolley and they all chatted for a while."

"Did you overhear anything interesting?" asked Terry.

"Someone brought up about the robberies. Don't forget Lady Fiona lives at Cadderly Manor, which was robbed. She said that the police are hopeless and she still hasn't had her art and valuables returned," said Lillian. "But then it got really interesting because one of the women whispered to another one that she reckoned she had probably sold them herself to pay for what she lost on the horses."

"That is interesting. It could be that Dora was threatening to tell her husband that she had a gambling problem. Don't forget Sir Edward has something to do with the government. If she was carrying out an insurance fraud and got found out, you're talking about prison time, not just shame. Is that it?"

"I can't think of anything else and I hate to tell you this, but they didn't mention my strawberry tarts!"

"I'm sorry to hear that, Betty. Jealousy is an awful thing. At least they didn't mention your apricot jam. Well done, you've both done really well," said Abigail.

"What shall we do next?" asked Lillian. "What about the names on that list?"

"I wish we could go and talk to them. It's a real bummer being dead sometimes. I guess Hayley will have to go. Terry and I could go to the Cricketers tomorrow at lunchtime and listen to what's going on. The landlord was one of the names and who else was?"

"The husband of beautiful Becks," said Terry.

"I might have known you would remember her," answered Abigail. If the truth be known, she felt a bit jealous. "Then it was Cassie Briggs and of course the major. I wonder if they have released him yet. I don't think it's him. That's far too easy."

"Perhaps he wasn't very good at murder. He's got the means, motive and opportunity," said Betty. "You know what they say, 'Where there's fire, there's smoke,'" she said seriously. "But don't you agree with me, Abigail, that all the evidence against him could be circumcisional?"

"Not exactly, dear Betty, I think it might be circumstantial though. Let's go round to Hayley's in the morning and plan our campaign to 'Free the Major', before Johnson charges the poor man."

"Isn't there anything we could do now?" asked Betty. "My mum used to say, 'Never do tomorrow today'… No, it was 'Never put off today for tomorrow … what you can do'… Hang on, it was 'Never put off until today what you can do…'"

Abigail was tempted to tell her that by the time she had got it right it would be tomorrow!

Hayley had been busy herself that evening. She had been to see

Shelley, the local vet earlier in the day, and found out the information that she needed. So not long after, she went to the small house in Windmill Lane and banged the large, brass door knocker.

"Mrs Bennett? I wasn't expecting you to call. Is anything wrong?"

Hayley lifted the fleecy blanket on the basket to reveal a furry, little ginger kitten. "The opposite, Janette. Can I come in? We need to talk."

Chapter 15

"So Tiggy was Tilly, wasn't she, Abi?" Hayley told Betty and Terry.

"What are the chances of that?" said Betty. "So what did Janette think of her new fur baby?"

"She started crying, so I wasn't too sure at first. But it was okay, they were tears of joy. It was love at first sight. She's going to call her Pumpkin because she's so orange."

"Perfect. Did you tell her what happened to Tiggy, or rather Tilly?" asked Abigail.

"I did. Not that I could tell her why she had passed. A car more than likely. She knew deep down that the worst had happened. Otherwise, Tilly would have gone home if she could have. I was going to say someone had told me they had seen a dead cat near the church a few months ago."

"Well, that's true, I did," said Abigail.

"I know, but we got talking. And before I knew it, I'd told her what I do and how I had found out. She was most interested. And I think we have another ally we can call on at times. She promised to keep it all to herself, and I believe her. We bonded over cats, actually. I even told her about the library, and she's just pleased that she's not imagining things. But I did promise you'll keep out of her way and not scare her."

"I'm glad for one," said Terry. "I was getting worried about a you-know-what getting called."

"Don't mention the ex word," said Betty.

"Like ex-boyfriends?" asked Abigail.

Betty looked deadly serious. "Nope. Ex like in exorcist. We have to watch out for them. Else, wham bam, we could be gone quicker than a hat in a hurricane."

Terry agreed. "I saw it once at an old house I had visited not long before. Must be about ten years ago. The new owners wanted to get rid of the old ones who thought it was still theirs, even if they were ghosts. And admittedly, they did some great haunting like pulling the bed covers off and trying to push them down the stairs. So it was kinda their fault. I'm not even sure it has to be a priest these days. But this one had them gone within half an hour."

"I wish they could do one on DCI Johnson. I'm sorry to tell you he's charged the major for Dora's murder."

"Johnson's charged him? You've got to be kidding me." Abigail couldn't believe what Hayley told them.

"Nope. He charged Major Cove last night. Tom told me all about it when he got home. The worst of it is, Tom is off the case and he's been sent to join Robbery. Johnson doesn't want him anywhere near Major Cove in case the Chief Constable thinks the arrest has got something to do with him. He's denying it, but without an alibi, he doesn't stand a chance. They found her bag and purse in his rubbish bin, which would have been taken away by the bin men this morning. He admitted to having an affair with Dora, but said it finished years ago when he refused to leave Esme. He broke the news to her in that posh hotel in Brighton. It triggered a lot of hate."

"Poor Dora," said Betty. "I know she wasn't very nice, but I don't like to think of her broken-hearted like that."

"She cheated on her husband for years though, hun, without a thought for his poor wife, Esme. Then when he died, she just assumed that Roland would move in with her, but that meant he would have lost all the money that his wife had. Dora wasn't poor, but the days of swanning around playing golf would have been over. But then she started blackmailing him a few years ago, going by his bank statements, Tom said. So you were right, Abi."

"But we know that he wasn't the only one. Aren't they going to look into the others? I think we should then. And then there's that ring that was locked away, so that must be something important. Terry and I are going to have a date at the Cricketers and see if we can find anything about the landlord, James Rich, aren't we, Terry? Lillian and Suzie are going to follow the cleaner, Cassie, around for some of her jobs. I wouldn't have thought that she earned enough to be blackmailed, but Dora might have used her to get information from the other houses that she cleans."

"That's a good idea. And I gave Cassie a call and said I need a cleaner and would she pop by for a chat. She's coming round later today," said Hayley. "First though, I thought I would pay a visit to Esme, to find out if she knows anything, but also to check that she is alright. I would have liked to put my feet up for a while. I haven't been sleeping well lately."

"Is it still that voice?" asked Abigail.

"It is. It woke me up about eight times last night and it's getting stronger. She's coming to me in my sleep, but I wake up and I can still hear her and Lou is definitely asking for my help, whoever Lou is. It may even be Lucy. Perhaps if I meditate she might come through."

"I've checked everywhere I can," said Terry. "There's no one that I can see. I went right round the church and all the places I can think of."

"That's another mystery for us then," said Abigail. "We'll get there. Don't forget our motto - All problems great and small. I hate to ask you, Hayley, but that just leaves Sexy Becksy and her husband, Mark. Do you think that you could think of an excuse to visit them tomorrow, or when you feel up to it? And before you ask, Terry, no you can't go!"

"I'm sure going to try. Just to see the look on Tom's face when I tell him!"

"I liked it when you said it was a date," said Terry, as they walked to the Cricketers Inn.

"It is kind of. Me and you going to the pub together. I would have had a large white wine. What about you? I'm buying."

"I'll have a pint of bitter, please. Although, in my day the woman wouldn't have paid for a thing, but I know it's different now. So I'll buy the meal. We'll have Chicken in a Basket."

"Blimey, that's going back a bit, Terry. Don't forget the prawn cocktail and the Black Forest gateau," she giggled.

"Chicken in a Basket was very popular in my day."

"Make it two then." Terry held his arm out, so she slipped hers through and they walked through the door.

It was a weekday lunchtime so there weren't many in there. Two men were sitting on stools at the bar and two couples were at either end of the room. James Rich was standing behind the bar chatting to the men. Abigail wasn't too impressed with him. He had slicked-back hair and was laughing loudly at his own jokes. Even she didn't do that - much, and her jokes were far funnier. Next to him was a young lady who was serving one of the men a pint of lager. She was about eighteen with long, dark hair and an innocent, nervous face. It was a job that Abigail had never fancied. She had once worked as a waitress part-time and she was pretty hopeless at that. She had always prided herself on a good memory, but it was shocking how many times she took the right food to the wrong person. Or was it the wrong food to the right person? She was never quite sure. They'd sacked her in the end. Not even in the end, she recalled. Two days actually. And forget the tips. It was amazing how no one tipped you when you accidentally spilled coffee on them. And she learned a lot of new words that day. She could only imagine if her customers were intoxicated as well as mad. No, a barmaid would not have been her job of choice.

Terry said how much the pub had changed since his day. The dartboard had gone and it looked more like a restaurant. Even the haze of cigarette smoke was missing. Abigail pointed to the wall where a poster was hanging, similar to the advert in the newspaper. "There's a pub quiz night soon, do you fancy coming?"

"Another date? I didn't know you cared. Why not? They didn't have them in my day. If I went to a pub it was to have six pints and pass out when I got home. How things change. What happens at a pub quiz then?"

"I haven't been to one for years. Each table thinks of a silly name and a quiz master reads out the questions. It says it's Julian Banning for this one. You write the answers down on one sheet of paper between you. It might be ten about history, then ten about sport or something. Then there's usually a few breaks so you can get a drink, and then at the end you hand in your answers, and the one with the most correct wins the prize. Sometimes it's money but often it's a bottle of wine, or even a beef joint or something."

"Seems a lot of hard work to me. And the people of today like them, do they?"

"They're very popular. Some people travel all around the villages to enter them," Abigail told him.

"Really? Everyone to their own, I suppose. Now if that was me and I took you on a date, I wouldn't bring you to any boring pub quiz. Sounds like going to school."

"So where would you take me, Terry Styles?"

"I'd call for you at your house, and bring you a posy of flowers from my garden. I'd even put my best suit on and polish my shoes. It would be perfect weather. Then you'd take my arm and we'd walk to the River Gore and hire a boat. I'd be an expert rower, of course."

"Of course."

"Then we would stop and tie the boat up, while I got out the picnic basket, and poured us a glass of champagne and we would eat chicken drumsticks and…"

"You like your chicken, don't you?"

"Don't interrupt. Chicken drumsticks and ham sandwiches. Then we'd lay on the blanket and look up at the blue sky while looking for shapes in the white clouds. You might have a little nap and I'd watch you sleep. Then we'd row downstream and watch the orange sun going down, with my arm around you like this."

"Then what?" Abigail wanted to know.

"Then I'd kiss you."

"And I would kiss you back." Their eyes locked until the spell was broken as a glass was dropped on the other side of the bar.

"Oh for God's sake!" said Terry. Talk about bad timing, he thought, and Abigail was none too pleased either.

The young woman returned with a dustpan and brush and bent over to sweep up the pieces. She immediately stood up and slapped James across the face and looked like she was going to cry.

"Whoa. I felt that," said Terry.

"That's the trouble with females today, they can't take a joke. Too much PC these days," James said, rubbing his cheek. He looked to the other men to agree with him, but they gave him a look of disgust and went to find a table.

"I told you if you ever touched me again, I'd let you have it. You can stick your job," said the young girl.

"You're fired anyway, darling. No one hits me."

"If he does that in front of people, imagine what he's like when no one is there to see. I think we can safely say what Dora held over him," said Terry. "He can go back to his slimy ways now she's out of the picture."

"We'll keep our eye on him at the quiz."

"On our date?"

"On our date."

Chapter 16

THE GRAVEL CRUNCHED UNDER HAYLEY'S FEET AS SHE walked up to Esme's front door. She wasn't sure if she would be welcome but had to try. She remembered that Esme was there when she was a guest speaker, doing one of her paranormal talks. But again, she had to decide if she should go as Hayley Bennett or Hayley Moon? Definitely, just Hayley.

Esme gave her a welcoming smile when she saw her and invited her in. She had visibly aged since Hayley had last seen her. The immaculately permed hair had a wild look to it and there seemed to be a lot more grey. Hayley felt sure that prior to this, she would never have answered the door wearing jogging bottoms.

"It's so nice to see someone. It's amazing how your friends disappear when your husband is arrested for the murder of his mistress, who's blackmailing him. Would you like a coffee? You go and sit outside and I'll bring it out."

It was a lovely garden and Hayley could feel that the two of them sat out there every morning and every afternoon, weather permitting. It had a wonderful view of Chittering Downs beyond, and several red kites were soaring above in search of their next meal. The very best of middle England, she thought.

She felt so sorry for Esme being ostracised by the rest of the village, through no fault of her own. Unless she had taken her husband's cravat and strangled Dora herself. The major was only guessing when he said it must have been stolen.

"Here we are, Hayley. Poor Roland. He loved sitting out here. He'll be missing his garden more than he's missing me, I suspect."

"It is a beautiful garden and a wonderful view. Have you heard how he is?"

"Nothing. His solicitor rang me to say he's been charged but not much else. I imagine he's taking it very badly. He was captured by the enemy when he was in the army, you know. So I don't suppose it would be as bad as that, but he must be missing his comforts terribly."

"Do you think he could have done it?"

"Not for a minute. He could bellow and bluster but not take a life. He saw too much of that during his time in the army and he lost many good friends. When I heard he had betrayed me with her, I would have loved him to get punished in some way, but not like this. For one thing, it's punishing me too. I can't sleep for thinking about him in that awful place. And as for that dreadful detective, I'm thinking of putting in a complaint."

"You should, Esme. If enough people do, perhaps the Chief Constable will do something about Johnson. Do you mind telling me what happened when you went to see Dora that evening? I swear I won't breathe a word to a living soul."

"It might help to talk about it. God knows I've gone through it in my head a million times. That woman told me in the most awful way. She let me sit down that night and blather on about committee meetings and expenses, and then came right out with it. She said, 'I hate to tell you, but Roland and I had an affair for three years. He's been paying me to keep it from you.

But now he hasn't got any money left, I might as well spill the beans.' Believe me, if I was going to kill her, I would have done it there and then. She looked so pleased with herself and actually laughed and told me what Roland likes in the bedroom. I stumbled out the door and came back here. I had to stay away from Roland when I got back. I think I would have taken a hatchet to his head if I had looked at him."

"Maybe don't say that to the DCI," joked Hayley. "She was a cruel woman, wasn't she? I don't suppose anyone deserves to be choked to death, but she comes close."

They sat in silence, drinking their coffee and enjoying the sunshine. Neither touched the biscuits that Esme had brought out.

Esme suddenly said, "I had no idea about the affair, you know. I expect people think that I did and was just a doormat, who behaved like a timid little mouse. But he would say he was meeting with his friends in the regiment, or off to play golf, and I let him get on with it. In actual fact, I was always glad of the peace and quiet. He could drive me up the wall sometimes. Men say women talk too much, but in my mind, they talk even more. Well, Roland did, and it wasn't usually something I was interested in. At the time, he was suffering from depression, looking back. He was more than likely bored, as he hadn't long retired from active duties. It's hard for a man to be disciplined in the army and then have so much time on his hands. I'm betting her husband didn't know either. That woman had us both fooled."

Hayley noticed that Esme couldn't bring herself to call Dora by her name. "If it helps, I haven't heard of one person in the village saying that they knew about the affair. It was a shock for everyone. So no one was talking about you behind your back."

"They are now, though. I bet I'm the talk of the town. In your capacity as a spiritualist, do you get any sense about Roland? Does any part of you think he could have killed that woman?"

"I would have to talk to him. But for what it's worth, I don't. There are just as many people who had a motive to want her dead. Between you and me, we think she was blackmailing others as well."

"The solicitor did tell me that. It doesn't surprise me, with her. Poor Roland. No wonder he was always broke. I gave him an allowance, and he could have asked me for more money at any time, but he didn't. He was old school like that. Thought a man should support the woman. Which is rubbish these days. He worked hard all his life, so I never minded helping him. But the thought that he was giving it to that floozy, and she was swanning about the village and behaving all pious at church, makes my blood boil." She turned away from Hayley, till she calmed down.

"Can you think of anyone Dora could have had a hold over?"

"The vicar, for a start. Why? I have no idea. Can't be fingers in the collection plate, there's not enough in there these days. And I don't think for a minute that he would do anything illegal. He would rather resign than pay her anyway. Then there's Lady Fiona Cummings, the previous head of the WI. Why else would she let her be in charge? We all think she likes the gee-gees a bit too much. I've seen her myself placing a bet on her phone. They make it so easy these days. She would never do it if she had to actually walk into a betting shop. Before she married Sir Edward, she lived in Norfolk, where her father bred race horses. It's in her blood, and I daresay she has always been addicted. Perhaps when this is over, I'll reach out to her. It's made me think about how we can ignore people and their problems. Sometimes a kind word and a bit of advice is all we need."

"That's so sweet of you, Esme, you're right. Can you see her strangling Dora, though?"

"If she was desperate enough, she might. She's got the build for it. I wouldn't like to take her on. And she would be mortified if the gentry of the county got to know her dirty little secret. Let alone her husband. When she was burgled, there were comments about her being the one to sell her things for the money and then claiming the insurance. And if she was paying that woman as well as her debts, then she would be very desperate indeed. Her husband, Sir Edward, has his career to think of. He's hoping to stand as a member of parliament one day, so she must be going through hell."

"That's very interesting. I don't know if you know, but my husband, Tom, is a policeman. Only uniform, in Robbery for now, but I could always put a word in his ear if you can think of anyone else."

"Is he? I didn't realise that. Well, I never. There was a nice young constable here when they were searching. He apologised and said he hoped they hadn't left too much of a mess. That has given me a bit of hope."

"That sounds like my Tom. Do you think you'll forgive Roland if he's exonerated? As much as I love my husband, I don't know if I could."

"I'm not sure, but he's only been gone a few days and I hate being on my own. The lesser of two evils, I suppose. And I've got used to our routine. We both had our hobbies. He had his golf, and he's an amateur radio ham. He'd spend many hours chatting away to far-flung places or tapping away on his morse key. Whereas I had my book club and enjoyed doing a bit of charity work and playing bridge. But we'd come together sometimes, like doing the gardening together or drives out in the country, or to the coast. Even meals at the local pub. I can't show my face in there at the moment. I went to the village shop yesterday, and no one looked me in the eye or spoke. I couldn't hear what they were saying, but half of them were thinking 'poor Esme', and the other half thought I was a crazed murderer, I expect. But God sends these things to try us. Not that I will go to church either. The congregation there are even more judgemental. The vicar did ring to see if I needed anything and said Mary would like to visit."

"Well, there you are, Esme. I'm very fond of Mary and I'm sure once the rest have got over the shock they will support you. It could just be a case of not knowing what to say. You have to stay strong. Have you got any family that you could stay with?"

"No, we didn't have children, more's the pity. I have a sister in Ireland, but she's one of those that you can't talk to at the best of times. To be honest, I'd rather stay in my own home."

"Now, excuse me for asking, but do you know anything about James Rich?"

"The landlord of the Cricketers? He's got more skeletons than the graveyard. Let's just say lock up your daughters and your granddaughters. He's very handsy, as my mother used to say. You should tell your husband to look into him."

"He has an alibi for Dora's murder, unfortunately. He was behind the bar."

"He still needs looking into. There's talk he gave a young barmaid a lift home after her shift one night and stopped in Ridgeway Woods on the way. Her parents rang the police, but it was a 'he said, she said', and he got away with it. At the very least, they could revisit the case."

"I doubt she was the first, Esme. Thank you for telling me. That's a great help. Now, another thing, does Cassie do your cleaning?"

"Cassie Briggs? No, I do it myself. Keeps me occupied. And the gardening, we both enjoy that. I must keep it tidy for when Roland comes home, but I can't say I'm in the mood to do anything. I'd rather stay in bed." She found a tissue out of her pocket and wiped her eyes. "I know it's pathetic, but I still love him."

"It's not pathetic. You're a kind, empathic person. There's no shame in that at all. You'll learn from this and whatever happens, it will help you in the future. To be there for others, for a start."

"It's true. Like poor Fiona. If this nightmare ever ends, I'll go and see her."

"One more thing," asked Abigail, "How well do you know Mark Jones?"

"Do you think he may have done it?" she said, shocked.

"Not really. But I did hear his name mentioned that Dora might have had her claws into him as well."

"He's a friend of Roland, although more a golf and drinking partner. It goes without saying he's a lot younger than him. I can't say that I've ever spoken to his wife. She's very beautiful, I do know that."

"So I've heard," said Hayley begrudgingly.

"That can be a curse as well. The other wives are perhaps not as friendly as they could be. They worry their husbands are going to pay more attention to her and jealousy is a wicked thing. Perhaps I could reach out to her. All I know about him is that he's the present captain of the golf club. If there has been any shenanigans going on there, I haven't heard. Roland says he's always flying abroad and sometimes has to cancel their round at the last minute. Whether that is suspicious, I wouldn't like to say. And I don't want to throw anyone under the bus for that Johnson to abuse, like he did me."

"You're one in a million, Esme. Roland is a lucky man. I'll be very careful what I say, I promise. And I definitely won't be giving any information to Johnson. I can't stand him either. Another name is Julian Banning."

"We've bought quite a few antiques and paintings from his shop over the years. Julian spends a lot of time in the Cricketers. I think he and the misogynistic Mr. Rich are best friends. One can only imagine what they talk about or get up to."

"I can imagine, and it's very unpleasant. We're not going to give up on Roland. I have some friends that are looking into the murder, and I'm sure he will be home and driving you up the wall again before you know it. Come on, let's eat these lovely chocolate biscuits before they melt."

Hayley left Esme's house with a feeling of lightness and her shoulders relaxed for a change. Not only had she made her feel better, but she had learned quite a bit about the case. She decided to pop to the library in case the rest of the gang were there. It was Janette's day off, and another librarian was in charge. He took no notice of Hayley as she walked around trying to find her friends.

The only ghostly one there was Betty, who was browsing the titles in the crime section. Hayley brought her up to date with what she had learned from Esme but kept the private revelations to herself. Even though she had promised not to tell a living soul, so in theory, she could have done.

"Poor Esme. How is she?"

"Surprisingly resilient. I think she'll make it. But it's even more important now to get the major released. I'm going to tell Tom about the slimy landlord. He shouldn't be able to get away with it."

"There's always been rumours, but running one of only two pubs in the whole village, he's been allowed to get away with it," said Betty.

"That's true. He thinks he's so omnipotent behind that bar."

"Was he now? That doesn't surprise me. At least my John never had that problem."

Hayley was going to explain, but she still had a busy afternoon ahead of her.

"If he touched one of my girls, John would have had his guts for garters. It's a wonder no one has killed him. Dora never goes in there anyway, so she wouldn't have worried about confronting him and asking for money. Don't forget he humiliated her when he asked her if she was Spanish."

"I'd forgotten about that. Oh, but he's got an alibi from

Cassie. Damn," muttered Hayley. "It's interesting what Esme said about Fiona Cumming."

"For all her airs and graces, she's no different to the rest of us. But it's an addiction so they say, I suppose. Maybe you should go and see her."

"I can't just knock on the door of Cadderly Manor, hun. But I could ring Lady Caroline to see if she could arrange tea at the Hall, and we both happened to be there. She'd love to be part of an investigation. I know she finds it most exciting." Hayley and the team had become friends with Caroline Hatton when they investigated a case at Chiltern Hall. She knew all about Abigail's help and their detective agency. She was the only living person that did, apart from Tom and now Janette.

"I'll give her a call later and ask. Then I could bring up the topic of addictions in front of Fiona and mention that I helped one of my clients with meditation or reiki. I'd love to do what I could for her. It must be hard to keep it to yourself. You'd think of nothing else night and day. Unless she's the killer, then she'll have to stop gambling when she's arrested."

"I've heard Sir Edward is very nice, so she should just tell him. They say a problem shared is a problem doubled or something. There's no need for her to suffer in silence because he's not short of a bob or two. He could easily cover her debts and get professional help. It must be a weight off her mind now that Dora is dead, don't you think?" she said knowingly. "Desperate measures call for desperate times, so they say."

Hayley often wondered who 'they' were that Betty had such great faith in!

"Absolutely. The list of suspects just keeps growing. I'd better get a move on. I've got Cassie Briggs and Rebecca and Mark Jones to see as well today. A psychic, private detective's work is never done!"

"I've got a bittersweet day myself tomorrow. I haven't said anything to the others, but it's my great granddaughter's birthday tomorrow. She's only five and they're having a little party for her at the church hall. It will be the first one that I've missed. John and I always went when there was one there. When it was at their houses we didn't. It was pretty much full up with the tots and parents. But everyone met up when it was in the hall. I used to help with the sandwiches, but as I got older they stopped asking for my help."

"Maybe they thought you had done enough over the years."

"I daresay you're right. But when you get to a certain age you can get a bit cranky about these things."

"So will you go tomorrow?"

"I think I will. I want to be there for the cake and when she blows out her five candles, I'll be there to help her. And when she makes her wish, I'll make my own for her."

"You can never have enough magic, hun. I'll say a prayer for her as well. Is her name River?"

"Yes, how did you know? Oh, I forgot who I was talking to."

"If it helps, I see nothing but light in her future."

"How wonderful. Thank you, Hayley. One does worry about them. My daughter, her nan, is sixty-three and I've never stopped worrying about her. It started the day she was born. And all the other children. But Angela was always the one I worried about most."

"Do you know, Betty, I can't say that I'm in any hurry to have children for that reason. Tom's not in any rush, thank goodness. I guess we all have Suzie now. It breaks my heart that she will never grow up to be the beautiful, black woman that she was destined to be. I find the kitten, Luna, enough of a worry. He's like our baby, and I can't imagine what we'd do if anything happened to him. Especially after what happened to Janette's cat. Although I don't suppose we will ever find out what caused Tilly to die."

"All the pets we had were one of the family, and I cried for every one of them when they passed over. Apart from the

Russian hamster they had, actually. That would take your fingers off if you touched it," laughed Betty. "But Luna is young so I don't think you need to worry. And cats have nine lives, so they say."

Hayley hoped 'they' would be right on that, if nothing else.

Hayley gave Tom a quick update by text when she got back home, just in case his boss was there. Then she nervously cleared her throat and rang Lady Caroline Hatton.

She was very happy to hear from Hayley, who brought her up to date with their investigations so far, and Caroline was more than happy to arrange a meeting between her and Lady Fiona Cummings.

"She's on some of the committees that I've been coerced into these days. When I was an actress in London, I never thought I would have to sit through them. My motto was 'never volunteer for anything'. I don't know which is more tedious, meetings or endless auditions. Actually, Hayley, you're in luck, I was at a dinner party last week and the Cummings were there. If she had troubles or was thinking of murdering someone, she never let it show. I sat opposite Sir Edward, so I'm sure I'll be able to think of a reason for her coming to tea."

"I would really appreciate it. Try and find out about the break-in she had as well."

"Someone else was talking about that. Apparently, they had it all insured for a lot more than it was worth. But we might all be guilty of that, I suspect. Fiona seemed rather nice, and I can't see her strangling that Dora, if I'm honest. But I'm not the best judge of murderers, as you well know. I'll do a bit more digging with some of the other women when I can. The ladies of the Pony Club are coming over later. They want me to open the old stable block, where they found that body. Apparently, I'm having the gymkhana here next spring. I don't even like horses. I've been scared to death of them since I got kicked on the knee when I was about ten. Honestly, I've never worked so hard in my life. And you don't get paid a dime!"

"Well, I won't feel too sorry for you," laughed Hayley. "I'm sure being Lady of the Manor and having millions in the bank has its compensations."

"When you put it like that, I've had worse days, I suppose," she conceded, with a giggle. "But the upkeep of this place is horrendous. That's without all the charity events I have to arrange. But I mustn't complain. How is The Deadly Detective Agency going?"

"Deadlier and deadlier. We're kept quite busy."

"It's terribly exciting. I'm glad to help anytime. So okay, Hayley, leave it with me and I'll let you know when Fiona is free and we'll get together. Cheerio for now."

Chapter 17

Hayley had only just finished her lunch when she heard the doorbell ring.

"Come in, Mrs Briggs. Thank you so much for coming round. I've been meaning to get a cleaner for ages." Cassie Briggs was a lot younger than she thought she would be. But she knew that she had been at school with Abigail, so she guessed that she was in her late thirties.

"I think I'm the only one in the village now. There's some big firms that come in from Gorebridge and work in groups of two or three, but you don't really know who's coming. With me, you get the personal touch and know you can trust me. I do all the big houses around here."

"That's good to know. So I could get a reference?"

"You could, but I've never had to give one before," she bristled.

"I'm sorry, Mrs Briggs, I didn't mean to insult you. It's just that you can't be too careful these days. Did you hear about Dora Bream? She was murdered in her own home, you know."

"I know that. I cleaned for her on a Friday morning. I had her key and used to do it for her while she went into Gorebridge. So

I've got a free space on a Friday if you want me to book you in. Although it doesn't look like you need a cleaner. Usually by the time they phone me there's a layer of dust and wall-to-wall cobwebs."

"You should see the other rooms," lied Hayley.

"And if you need a gardener, my son Chris can help you out. He's a lot cheaper than the others around here. They call themselves landscape gardeners and charge double the price."

"My garden is tiny, so even I can manage that. We had a conservatory put in, and that halved it. Thank you anyway. Are you free on a Saturday, like late afternoon? Fridays wouldn't really work for me." Hayley thought she was getting good at this sleuthing.

"Sorry, I can't do Saturdays. I work part-time in the Cricketers. From four till closing."

"You do work hard."

"I like it there. The boss is a bit of a creep, but I enjoy the banter." Hopefully, Tom had checked her alibi for the night of the murder.

"Can I think about it and let you know?" Hayley said, getting to her feet.

"I hope you do. It's a lot cleaner than my other ones. If I didn't know better, I might think that you'd got me round here under false pretences. You're not a reporter, are you? Or a private investigator looking into the murder? You're too late if you are, they've arrested the old major. And in case you were wondering, we've got alibis. I was in the pub working, and my son was in a pub in Gorebridge, so don't get any ideas," she snapped and stood up, towering over Hayley.

"A private investigator?" Hayley scoffed. "Whatever next. I'm a therapist of sorts, actually."

"I did wonder when I saw all the crystals and that. Sorry if I offended you."

"Not at all. It's quite funny, actually. I will definitely be in touch if I get a cleaner. You're at the top of my list." Hayley breathed a sigh of relief when she closed the door on her. She would need to be more careful in the future. If Cassie had been the murderer, chances were she could have been her next victim. Tomorrow she was going to see Mark and Rebecca Jones, and she had better think of something that didn't get her killed.

Suzie and Lillian had done a stakeout for Hayley to see what time Mark usually got home from work the previous day. Hayley hoped to time it right so that she could have a private word with the lovely Rebecca before he came back. Or kill two birds with one bush as the adorable Betty had put it. She had made an extra effort to look nice and styled her long black hair. She even put on make-up and lipstick, but she still wore one of her long flowing skirts that she was known for. She wasn't much older than Rebecca, but she felt it today, as according to Terry, she was Becklesfield's answer to Marilyn Monroe.

There was only one car on the driveway, so Hayley assumed she was on her own. Rebecca opened the door with a smile and a seductive look in her eye. It soon disappeared when she saw her visitor was a woman from the village.

"Oh. What do you want? I've already given to the church."

"It's Rebecca, isn't it? I'm letting the ladies of the village know, who aren't members of the WI, that I'll be a guest speaker at a meeting, and they are welcome to come."

"What is it this time? Vegan jam making?"

"It's not all scones and quiches these days. I gave a talk not long ago, and it was a full house. I'm a psychic medium and...."

"Wow. You're not that amazing Claire Voyant from the paper, are you? I was going to phone you to have my palm read."

"I certainly am not! I'm Hayley Moon, and I've had the gift since I was six."

"I'm sorry. Would you like to come in, please?" begged Rebecca. The overt sexiness had disappeared, and underneath was an excited young girl. "Do you see dead people? Sometimes

I see shadows around the village. I did yesterday, you know. I'm sure they're always among us."

"That is interesting that you can see things, because I happen to know that Becklesfield is a bit of a hotspot for the dead. There are more about than you think actually."

"So tell me about your talks. I'd go to one of them, they sound fascinating."

"Last time it was in the Church Hall, and there were a lot of people there. I explain what I do, like readings, faith healing, about angels and all things paranormal. Then I take any questions, and at the last one, I gave a message to a lady from her father and unwittingly told the whole village that she was expecting a baby. Unfortunately, before she'd had a chance to tell her family. We had a bit of a laugh about things as well. And of course, it all ended with tea and cakes. You'll love it if you're already interested in the subject. Sounds like you're a bit of a sensitive yourself, but you're safe here though. I don't sense any angry spirits in your house at the moment. But with a murder happening so close, I can understand if you're a bit worried."

"Are you telling me you know that the murderer is going to kill again and that it's going to be here?" Rebecca said intently.

"Good Lord, no. I just meant if Dora was still earthbound and was seeking vengeance."

"God, I never even thought of that. She won't be coming here then. I might get up to a few things that I shouldn't, but murdering old ladies isn't one of them. There are a few men in my past that I could happily throttle, but no old women."

"What about your husband?"

"Oh, I could definitely throttle him."

"No," said Hayley, laughing. "Would she come here if he had done it?"

"Mark? Are you sure you're a psychic? He wouldn't kill anyone. He puts a fly or a spider under a glass and then chucks it out the door. Plus, he was away on a business trip when she died. He didn't like her, though. I saw him talking to her a few times outside the gate, and they never looked like friendly chats. I heard them once when I was coming out of the front door, but it was just about the golf club funds, and he told her where to go. I thought it odd because she never even played golf as far as I knew. But that's what the busybodies are like around here. Not that they give me the time of day."

"Not all the women are like that. Most of them are very kind. Give the WI a chance. On the whole, they're lovely and do so much for the village. Take Mary Stevens, the vicar's wife; she's not much older than you and she's great fun. She'd be more than happy to go for a drink and introduce you to some other youngsters."

"I'll think about it. I'm going crazy stuck in here. I thought when I met Mark I was so lucky and I'd got everything I'd ever wanted - the man, the house, the money. I seem to be losing the man, and the house is my prison. Even the money doesn't seem to be as important as when I didn't have any."

"I hope you don't mind me saying, but I do sense that you are very lonely, even if you have everything that you always dreamed of when you lived in the flat, above the butcher's shop with your dad."

"Amazing. How could you have known that?"

Hayley ignored her. "You even make passes at men you're not interested in, just for a bit of company. I can even sense a young policeman that came here recently," she slipped in.

"Yes, the nervous police constable. He was super cute. But said he was happily married. The nice ones always are."

Hayley knew she would have to spoil Tom tonight. "The main thing I'm getting is that you really love your husband."

"I do, but all he ever does is work and play golf, and sometimes he goes to Amsterdam or Paris for days on end and always says I can't go with him. Talk of the devil, here he is."

A tall, fair-haired man with beautiful green eyes came

walking into the hall, while shouting out to his younger wife. "Hi, Becks. Is dinner ready, sweetheart? I've got a meeting at the… Oh, sorry, I didn't know we had company."

"This is Hayley Moon. She's trying to get me to join in village life and maybe the Women's Institute."

"I'm afraid you're wasting your time there. I've tried many times, and I'm not sure the Women's Institute would be prepared for my wife either," he said with a smile on his face, which made Hayley realise what Rebecca saw in him.

"That's where you're wrong, Mr Jones. They need youth and new skills to carry it forward. I'm sure there's a lot they could learn from her."

"I'm sure there is," he joked as he kissed the top of her head. "I'm all for my wife making new friends, as long as they're women, of course. So are you like an army recruiter or something?"

"Not really, I was hoping that Rebecca would come to one of my talks on the supernatural."

"I was not expecting that. Sounds very interesting. I'm into that kind of thing myself."

"Hayley was just talking about Dora, and we were wondering if her soul was floating around looking for her killer."

"God, I hope not. She was enough trouble when she was alive."

"Was she? In what way?" asked Hayley.

"Sticking her beak in things that didn't concern her. I can't say I'm sorry that Roland killed her, and I can fully understand why he did. Although, I'm going to miss him for our rounds of golf on the weekend."

"There are doubts about his guilt."

"Really? I thought he'd been charged." Mark looked a bit worried.

"But he hasn't admitted to it, so investigations are ongoing." She didn't say that it was only by The Deadly Detective Agency.

"Anyway," Hayley added with a sweet smile, "I'm sure she won't come after you. Between us, they do say that Dora might have been blackmailing people."

Rebecca thought that was hilarious. "No. I didn't think she had it in her. Perhaps this village isn't as dull as I thought. Come on then, give us the juicy gossip. Who and what had they done? Let me guess... Miss Spittle. She said I'd only given her a tenner. And I wouldn't trust that bloke who runs the pub either."

Mark felt he had to stop her. "I don't believe it for a minute. And we can't go around accusing people, darling."

"Mark's right. It's only a theory the police are working on. So don't spread it about. Now listen, it's not Dora, but I do feel an older woman is in the room with us. Does the name Rita mean anything to either of you?"

"That was my mother's name," said Mark.

"Grey hair in a bun and wearing a kaftan?"

"Good Heavens, that certainly sounds just like her," he said in amazement. "We lost her a few years ago before we got married, so she never met Rebecca. What's she saying?"

"She says she's disappointed in you. She says you've got a lovely, beautiful wife who loves you, but you spend more time in that damn golf club than you do with her. If you don't show her the love and kindness she deserves, you're going to lose her and your future family."

"Wow. My mum said that? I will, Mum, I promise." Mark sat next to Rebecca on the sofa and took her hand. "I'm sorry, sweetheart. From now on, I'll spend more time at home. I'll cancel the meeting tonight. The golf club will carry on without me."

It was an altogether different Rebecca she left to the one that answered the door. Hayley smiled to herself as she walked down the path. "Sorry, Rita. It's for the best. You'll see. His two daughters and one son will be the making of him." What Rita had actually asked Hayley to pass on to her son was, "When you see your father, tell him his new wife spent two thousand pounds on that coat, not the eighty she told him. And, oh yes, tell him she's having an affair with her hairdresser!"

She walked home in a happy daze, and hoped Tom wouldn't be late home tonight as she was going to chill some wine and get two nice, big steaks out of the freezer. And what the hell - she'd even find out her sexy underwear. He'd told the best-looking female in the county that he was happily married. Hopefully, it would still fit after all this time. But then she heard the female voice as clear as day and this time she definitely wasn't dreaming.

Hayley had walked as far as the shops when she heard it again. This time it was louder and she could clearly hear that it was calling her name and begging for help. Hayley walked towards the voice, but every time it got further away. It was like she was being led somewhere. She wondered if she would be coming across her body. It wouldn't be the first time. That had been in a wood and in a place where no one would have found the young man. But this time she was nearing a group of grey flint houses on the other side of Becklesfield. As she got closer, she realised it was the cottage with the blue door that was beckoning her. The voice confirmed it by saying, 'Here'. She had no doubt there would be a woman's body in there, hopefully dead of natural causes and not brutally murdered. She got out her phone to ring Tom, but then saw something that made her change her mind.

Chapter 18

A MAN WAS LOOKING AT HER THROUGH THE BAY window. She knocked loudly and wondered who he was and why he hadn't called the police. "Don't say it's another murder." But as he opened the door, she finally understood and realised who it was that needed her help.

"Have you found her?" he asked. "My wife, Lucy, has gone missing. She went to work on Friday and hasn't come home. No one will tell me anything."

Hayley walked in and shut the door behind her.

"Please help," said the lady's voice again. Hayley whispered she would and blinked away the tears in her eyes as she followed him into the house. "Help my Matthew."

The elderly man, in an old green cardigan, shuffled slowly in his worn slippers to a wing-backed chair. Hayley didn't think she had ever seen anyone so thin. There was no fat on his bones, let alone muscle. He could have been any age between sixty and ninety. "Have they found my Lucy yet? I'm so glad someone has come at last."

"Hello, Matthew. My name is Hayley, and I know where she is, and she's fine. Don't worry about her. She's exactly where she should be. But I think we should help you first. You look like you could do with something to eat. Let me go and put the kettle on and get you a nice cup of tea. You sit there. I'll make it."

Hayley went into the kitchen and took in the sorry mess. Plates and cups were stacked up on the sink, and the table was covered with stale food. "Lucy, can you tell me about Matthew?" She still didn't appear, but Hayley could hear her voice.

"I died four months ago of a sudden heart attack. It was a real shock for everyone, but especially for Matthew. He was perfectly alright until after the funeral. Sad, of course, but putting on a brave face. I think keeping busy helped; there was so much to sort out. Then gradually, friends and family stopped visiting. I've watched him sleep in that chair for weeks, never going to bed. And he's stopped washing himself and never takes off that old green cardy that I told him to throw out years ago. He just sits in the window and never bothers eating. Matthew refused to throw away any of my belongings and clothes. Just kept saying he wasn't ready and would do it next week. It could have been delayed shock, but he got more mixed up as time went by. Looking back, I think he had already started to get confused before I died. Just little things, like he'd repeat himself and when we talked about our daughter, he would ask the next day why I hadn't told him."

"My grandmother had Alzheimer's too. It was an awful time for everyone. She didn't recognise my grandad and used to ask who he was. She remembered him as he was when they first met. I think your husband is thinking of you as you were when you were young and has forgotten that you died. Or his mind doesn't want to remember that you did. It's so sad. He must have been in such a turmoil thinking you hadn't got home from work safely. Is there someone I can call?"

"My daughter lives in Scotland. I would be so grateful. She tried to get him to move up there with her, but he always was stubborn. Her phone number is in the address book in the hall, next to the phone. Her name is Linda Conway. Tell her I love her when you talk to her. I feel I'm getting weaker and have to cross over again. You will help, won't you?"

"Don't worry anymore, Lucy. I'll ring Linda now, and get Matthew something to eat." All was quiet, and Hayley knew Lucy had gone. There was no bread or food in the fridge, but she managed to find some biscuits and tinned meat. She took it into Matthew, who looked apprehensive.

"Who are you?" he asked in a frightened voice. "How did you get in?" Hayley explained and realised how serious it was when he asked who Lucy was.

"I'm going to ring your daughter, Linda, to come and visit you."

"Little Lindie? Good. I'd like to see her. It's about time she got home from school. Where's Lucy? She'll be pleased. Can you go and tell her? She must be upstairs or in the garden."

"She already knows, Matthew. Don't worry."

Linda was shocked to hear how quickly her father had gone downhill and said she would get the train down first thing in the morning. She also said she would ring her son who lived an hour away to stay with him until she arrived. Hayley explained that she was a neighbour who had popped in to see him and found him frail and confused, but she would stay with him until help arrived. Linda said she had bought a smallholding in Scotland and there was plenty of room for him to move in. She was very grateful but was as confused as her father when Hayley told her that her mother, Lucy, sent her love.

It was nearly dark when Hayley got home, but Tom was on a late shift, so she had plenty of time. She got out the steaks and laid the table to surprise him for behaving so well when confronted with Sexy Becksy.

But before she could squeeze into the black lace bodysuit

with the pink frills, she got a text from him. Chiltern Hall had been burgled. So don't wait up.

Hayley did wait up. She always liked to know that he was home safe and sound before she slept. But that night, it was more she wanted to know what was going on that kept her watching out the window for his car. "Watch out, Luna," she joked to her little kitten. "Curiosity killed the cat. And you're already down to eight lives." Luna wasn't worried; he just purred and enjoyed the late-night tickles. It was past two o'clock when Tom came in the front door.

"What happened, hun? Is Caroline okay?"

"Hello, Tom. How was your day?" Tom said sarcastically.

"I'm sorry. But I only spoke to her earlier today. We even talked about the robbery at Cadderly Manor. I can't believe it."

"She is a bit shocked that someone could get in that easily, but not too bad. She went to bed early and didn't hear a thing. It always amazes me that the rich in these big mansions don't have better security. Why don't they have a guard patrolling at night or something?"

"Money, I expect. Can you imagine the upkeep on these huge houses? She was just talking about that today. The heating and electricity alone must be horrendous. Then there's the gardeners and cleaners to pay. Did they take much?"

"No, surprisingly. Inspector Hudson said they seemed to know what to target and it was mostly small things. The other robberies, like at the Cummings' place, large paintings and ornaments were taken as well as valuables, but this was more of a smash and grab. They broke a pane of glass in the French window to reach the handle and only took stuff from the drawing room. Lady Caroline said the only things that were missing that she could tell were a Japanese plate, a pair of 18th-century duelling pistols off the wall, and a small religious painting, I think it was called an icon, that was priceless and irreplaceable. He thought it could be a theft to order, maybe a collector."

"What time did it happen?"

"Sometime before midnight. Lady Caroline would never have heard it in that huge house. Her and Mrs. Bittens, the housekeeper, were the only ones there. The cook was away for a few days at her daughter's house in Wales. We've checked and don't think she was involved. Mrs. Bittens went down to get a drink of milk and saw the door was open. She must have just missed them. Otherwise, we wouldn't have been called out until tomorrow. Which would have suited me. I'm absolutely shattered."

"No fingerprints on anything, or blood on the broken glass like on the TV?"

"Unfortunately not. In and out in two minutes, the Inspector reckoned. Not a lot of hope of seeing the stuff again either. By the way, keep tomorrow night free, Hayl. Dave and Isabella Mills want us to make up a four for the pub quiz at the Cricketers. Should be a laugh. We could do with a night out and, oh yeah, when you texted me this afternoon, you said you had a treat for me, what was that?"

Hayley looked down at her fleecy pyjamas, socks, and old cosy dressing gown. "Uh, nothing. Sorry, hun. Had your chance, muffed it."

Chapter 19

TOM HAD TO LEAVE EARLY THE NEXT MORNING AS A meeting had been called for the robbery squad, and even the superintendent was going to sit in on it. Too many wealthy and influential people had been targeted, including Sir Edward Cummings at Cadderly Manor and now the Hattons of Chiltern Hall. The Chief Constable himself had told them to forget everything else and concentrate on the high-profile break-ins. The young constable was enjoying it far more than working with Johnson. Inspector Hudson was as different as you could get to him. He treated the uniforms with the same respect as he did the top brass, and his men in return did the same for him and gave him their best work and extra time.

Inspector Hudson sat on the edge of a table at the front, with Superintendent Cross sitting on a chair to his right. He was giving the details of the thefts and was showing crime scene photographs of the entry points. In all the cases except Chiltern Hall, obscured doors had been jimmied open. The culprits seemed to know where the cameras were in advance, pointing to inside help. Interviews with staff had taken place to no avail.

Next, a collection of photos for insurance purposes were handed around. The prices elicited a few gasps from the uniforms.

"Are you sure it's not them doing it themselves for the insurance money? It's got to be tempting. Three thousand pounds for a painting of a windmill and a river? Crazy," said WPC Jane Nichols.

"If it was just one of them, maybe. But the aristocracy who've been targeted don't need the money for a start, and Sir Edward would have too much to lose."

A photograph of a black enamel and gold brooch was passed to Tom, valued at one thousand pounds. Tom's heart skipped a beat. He knew how important this was.

"Sir. I've seen this." He walked up to the front and passed it to the Inspector, and the superintendent stood up.

"You've seen this brooch?"

"Yes, Sir. You see, it's not just a brooch. It's a Victorian mourning brooch, and inside it is a lock of hair from a deceased person."

"Oh yeah? How do you know that?"

"Because I was going to buy it for my wife, but it was over eight hundred pounds and also had someone's hair in it. It was in Banning's antique shop in Becklesfield."

"Great observation, Constable," said the superintendent. "That is the first real break we've had."

Hudson agreed. "Well done, Tom. But it doesn't mean he had anything to do with the robberies. He might have just bought it innocently from somewhere, even at an auction. But once we know where from, we'll have a lead. Look up what we have on Banning, and if you find anything dodgy, we'll get a warrant and search his shop."

"Funnily enough, Sergeant Mills and I are going with our wives to a pub quiz tonight in the village, and he's running it. Well, he's the quizmaster."

"Great. Keep an eye on him. See if he has any conversations

with anyone out of the ordinary. You really should put in for your sergeant's exam. You'll go far, Bennett."

"Tell Tom well done from us. That is very interesting," said Abigail. "We have a new suspect at last, Julian Banning." Abigail, Terry, Betty, and Hayley were enjoying the sunshine and sitting on the village green. "Does anyone know him?"

"I knew his father," said Betty. "He was the original owner of the shop. I used to buy things there. Horse brasses were very popular in the eighties for some reason. We had them all around the fireplace."

"So did we," said Lillian. "I think Julian has been running it for a good ten years. It's gone a bit upmarket these days. My mum and dad used to go there when I was little and buy chests of drawers and things, but they wouldn't be able to afford anything there now."

Hayley nodded. "Tom said it was very expensive, the jewellery especially. But there were no customers when he was there. A lad who worked there was, but no one else. I wonder if he sells much. It could be he's been buying stolen goods because his shop is in trouble. He has a lot of dark wooden furniture and that isn't so popular now."

"Gives him a great motive for Dora's murder if she found out what he's been up to," said Abigail.

"I wonder how she knew. Didn't Tom say they found a man's ring from there in her house? We thought she might have bought it for the major, but what if she saw it in there and recognised it from the robberies at one of the houses. Maybe even remembered someone wearing it."

"Then bought it to threaten Banning. Good catch, Terry. You're right. So she went in there for some reason, like seeing something she wanted in the window, saw the ring and bought it. Then, either then or sometime later she said something like, 'It's funny, so-and-so had one stolen just like this a few weeks ago. But don't worry, I won't say a word if you pay a thousand pounds to the Amber Road Bird Sanctuary'."

"He might have decided there and then to kill her. We'll have to ask Tom if there's a date on it because she was outside having an argument that day, so maybe she had been in there."

Betty added, "And he was going home when he saw Esme Cove coming out of Dora's, so he thought she would be a good… what's the word? Skatecoat."

"She would be, her or her husband. Tom said Julian had seen Dora arguing with the major in the past. And if he overheard about the affair or the blackmail then, either would do to get the blame. So he either slipped in then or later. Is there a back way to get into her house, Terry?"

"Yes, there is. If you go down the lane by the park, it runs along there. He could get over the fence where the orchard is. No one would see."

"Oh, I do hope we can get Roland released," said Betty. "For Esme's sake as well. She might even forgive him after what he's been through. It was nearly ten years ago, after all."

"We need more than that though. If Tom can see a picture of the ring on the insurance claims, that will help. One stolen item is a coincidence, but two could be a pattern," said Abigail.

Terry said, "I bet after he strangled her he…."

"Oh no," said Abigail, holding her head. "You've just reminded me. Whoever killed her had already stolen the major's cravat to frame him. It would have been premeditated, so he can't have decided to do it that night, although he could have thought that was the perfect time when he saw Esme flouncing out of there. We'll have to do a lot more thinking before we let Johnson know."

"As I was saying before I was rudely interrupted," said Terry. "After he strangled her, I bet he tried to find that ring and couldn't open that drawer. He couldn't afford to stay there that long so was going to go back on Sunday. He wouldn't think that someone would miss her and check on her."

Abigail let out a big sigh and said, "Now, prepare yourself for a shock, everybody. I might have been wrong about something."

"That's not a shock," said Terry. "It's a shock that you're admitting to it."

"Charming. Do you remember when I said that Dora was cutting letters out of the newspaper to blackmail someone? For one thing, she got pleasure in letting them know that she knows, so didn't want to hide her identity, but also I think she may have been cutting out one of the other things now. If her death is connected to the burglaries, then perhaps she was cutting out the article about the robbery at Cadderly Manor, letting Banning know that she knew he was responsible for all the thefts even. If he was that involved, he would certainly need to shut her up."

"We'll let you off, dear," said Betty. "I think you've made up for it. Would he be able to do it on his own though? I can't imagine him dressing in black and getting into houses through the windows like a common burglar."

"Nor me, so we'll have to find out who his friends or acquaintances are."

Hayley looked at her watch and stood up. "Sorry, folks, I'm out with Tom and Dave Mills tonight. I daren't be late. Let's meet at mine in the morning. Not too early, eleven is fine."

"Okay," said Abigail. "Let's all have a think how we can prove that Julian Banning is a cold-hearted murderer."

Chapter 20

HAYLEY NOTED THAT THERE WERE SEVEN OTHER QUIZ teams on tables, all hoping to win the luxury hamper from Hardings. She wasn't bothered about what was inside; she just wanted to win. She was so laid back about most things, but put a tennis racquet in her hand or challenge her to a race, and she turned into Serena Williams or Usain Bolt. It wasn't so much that she hated to lose; it was more that she really, really wanted to win. Her mother always liked to bring up the stories of her birthday parties, the ones when they had to pause the music on her every time they played 'pass the parcel'. And they might as well stop the party if she didn't win 'musical statues'. She liked to think she wasn't quite as bad as that these days. She probably wouldn't even start crying and stamp her feet if she didn't win tonight. Whoever said it was the taking part that counts was an idiot in her eyes.

The four of them had decided on the name The Fiddling Four, for no particular reason other than it sounded good. Hayley really liked Dave's wife, Isabella. They had been to dinner at their house a few times as they had a small daughter, so it was easier to go there. The two ladies had decided to share a bottle of white wine, while the two men had pints of lager in front of them.

Hayley took a sip and looked to see what the competition was like. A few of the other tables looked like they were taking it very seriously. One lot was even studying general knowledge textbooks. Now that was taking it a bit too far. Hayley was so pleased to see that Mark and Rebecca were sitting at a table. They were looking into each other's eyes and holding hands. Surely Rita wouldn't mind her little white lie. Beverly Hobbs, Shirley Dawkins, Harry Harding, and Miss Spittle also made up a team and sat near the bar, all enjoying a sherry.

Hayley stared at James behind the bar and saw him in a different light after what Esme had told her. She would keep an eye on him tonight, and if he even looked at a woman a bit funny, she'd say something. She saw that Cassie Briggs was working behind the bar next to him, but she knew she'd be able to take care of herself. And going by what Esme had said, she was too old to be of interest to him anyway. The bar was two deep with customers, so Cassie really had her hands full. Everyone was trying to get their drinks before the quiz started. A boy with curly hair was trying to get her attention. Hayley heard her say, "Not now. Just go. I'll see you at home later." Must be her son who does the gardening, thought Hayley.

She looked towards the door and nearly choked on her wine. That was all she needed. What the hell were they doing here? How could she concentrate and win the quiz with them hovering about and talking to her?

"Ooh, ooh," shouted Abigail and waved when Hayley caught sight of her. "You didn't tell us you were going to be here."

"No, I..." She forgot for a second that no one else could see Abigail and Terry, and to them, she would be talking to herself. "...really like this wine." Hayley raised her eyebrows a few times and jerked her head to tell them to go. Isabella raised her own and wondered if she had developed a twitch.

"I'm just going to the bathroom before we start. Won't be a sec," said Hayley as she gave Abigail a dirty look and crossed the packed bar.

Once inside and after she had checked under the stalls, she said, "What on earth are you and Terry doing here? How can I think of the answers if I've got you two chattering in my ears?"

"Sorry, I'm sure. For your information, Terry and I are on a date and we had no idea you'd be here."

"A date? I'm very pleased for you, but do you have to have it here?"

"Terry's never been to a pub quiz, so we're only going to sit and watch and see how we do. You never know, we might beat you. You kept it very quiet about coming. Anyone would think you didn't want us here."

"And they'd be right! I love a good pub quiz, as long as I win. Not only that, Tom and Dave are here to keep an eye on Julian. Just in case he talks to anyone about the robberies. I think I'll check out the shop myself tomorrow and see what vibes I get off him."

"Well, be careful and good luck with the quiz. But we're going to wipe the floor with you. You're going down, Hayley Bennett," teased Abigail.

"As if. The Fiddling Four have got this in the bag. Now stay out of my way, please. Most of Becklesfield already think I'm nuts because I talk to myself, so I was rather hoping Isabella wouldn't see that side of me for a while longer."

"Scouts' honour, Hayl. We'll sit on the other side and whisper. You won't even know we're here." Hayley would have liked to believe that, but somehow she doubted it.

Fifteen minutes later, Julian Banning was sitting on a stool in front of the bar. He had a pint of beer next to him on a small table and the first set of questions in his hand.

"Ladies and gentlemen, thank you for coming and good luck to everyone. All of the entry fees and profits will go to our own

'Wet & Wildlife' charity shop. So dig deep for all the little animals that we are so lucky to have around our beautiful village. There's a tin next to me here, for you to put any donations in, and I'll give it to the manager, Harry, at the end of the night. So please be generous. I hope you've all turned your phones off and they aren't out in front of you. Not that any of you would cheat. Except maybe you, Bob," who seemed to be in on the joke.

"Have you all written the name of your team at the top? Good. General knowledge is the first round. Question one. Which sport is featured in the 2003 film, Seabiscuit?"

Dave had been elected to write down the answers, although Hayley was hoping she'd be able to. He wrote 'Horse racing' before she could even tell him.

"Question two. Which Scrabble letter is worth five points?"

She was about to whisper the answer to Dave when she heard Abigail shout out, "I know this one - K." By then, Tom had told Dave it was K. She glared in their direction, but they were not looking her way.

"Three. In which county is Blenheim Palace?" Hayley and Isabella both said Oxfordshire at the same time. The next six questions were straightforward. Dave knew a heptadecagon has seventeen sides and a dice has 21 spots. The ladies knew Batman's butler was called Alfred and Wolverine was played by Hugh Jackman. But they could only guess how many eggs Cool Hand Luke had eaten.

"Here's the tenth and last question in this section and then we can all refill our glasses. Who played the ghost in the 1947 film, The Ghost and Mrs Muir?"

All three of her teammates immediately turned to Hayley. "How the hell would I know that?" she told them.

Tom gave her a puzzled look and whispered, "Because you're a bloody psychic. You must know. It's about a ghost."

"How old do you think I am? It's a bit before my time." Then she heard Terry shout out, "I know. I went to the pictures to see it. Rex Harrison. That's who it is."

"Rex Harrison," said Hayley to her very impressed team. She didn't look over at Terry or Abigail, so they wouldn't know that she had technically cheated. "Pass me the bottle, Isabella. This is harder work than I thought it would be."

Tom and Dave went to the bar to get their pints, where it was packed with customers trying to catch the eye of Cassie or James. Hayley hoped they were buying another bottle of wine for them; she had a feeling that she was going to need it. Ten minutes later, the rush was over, and Hayley watched as James, the landlord, went over to give Julian another drink. "Here, I've poured you a brandy, your favourite brand. Thanks for doing this, mate."

"No problem. Just keep the drinks coming." He put the brandy next to the half-full glass of beer. Hayley locked eyes with the landlord as he turned, and she felt a feeling of heaviness and thought, this man is cold and evil. How evil, she wasn't sure. Julian went off to talk to friends for a few moments then called for quiet and had a swig of his pint of beer. The next round was going to be a favourite of Tom's - history.

"Question eleven. What year did Edmund Hillary and Tenzing Norgay reach the summit of Everest?"

Tom screwed up his face. He knew it was in the fifties. When was it? He hoped he'd get it before Dave did, seeing as he had told them how good he was at history. If they lost because of him, he'd never live it down at work. Hayley heard Terry shouting out the answer and repeated it in a low voice, "1953, hun."

He took the pen off Dave and wrote it down quickly as time was running out. He just hoped she was right. So did she, but Terry had seemed pretty sure. After all, he was there at the time.

"Question twelve." Julian reached for his beer and took

another mouthful. "What was the name of Agatha Christie's first book?"

Hayley was relieved that Tom knew the answer was The Mysterious Affair at Styles. Even if she was a detective, she had no idea. Of course, Abigail knew it as well, but she shouted out the answer, evidently forgetting all about her promise to whisper. Everyone turned around as a young couple entered the pub, who had no idea there was a serious pub quiz going on, as everyone glared at them. They walked quietly to the bar and apologised.

"Question thirteen." Julian finished off his beer before saying, "What is the breed of dogs famous for sea rescues in Canada?" They all agreed that it was Newfoundlands. Funnily enough, there was complete silence from Hayley's two friends. Ha, got you, she thought.

Julian picked up his brandy glass between his fingers and swirled it around, before having a sip. "What is the name given to…." A horrible gurgling sound came from his throat. The papers were thrown in the air, and Julian Banning fell off the stool and onto the floor. By the time Sergeant Mills had bent down to help him, the quizmaster was already dead.

Chapter 21

THE LAST PERSON ABIGAIL AND TERRY WANTED ON their date night was Detective Chief Inspector Johnson. Not that he wanted to be there either. Especially when he saw PC Bennett and that weird wife of his were as well.

"Mills, with me. Bennett, stand at the door and don't let anyone leave."

"We haven't let anyone out, Sir. Everything's left as it was when it happened."

"Forensics will be here soon, so you'd better move the witnesses to the other bar and start taking their names and addresses. Right, Sergeant, who is he and why are you two here? I didn't realise you two were such good friends. I'm not sure I like that." Abigail and Terry were standing right next to them. They wouldn't miss this, and they were wondering why as well.

"Me and Tom were coming for the quiz anyway, but also to keep our eye on the deceased."

"Didn't do much good then, did you? So who is he?"

"Julian Banning, who owns the antique shop here in Becklesfield. We questioned him about the Bream murder. He was seen going past her house that night, and also she had an argument with the major right outside his shop. Bennett questioned him about it, and he said he hadn't heard a thing. But the strange thing is that his name came up in one of the burglaries, the one at Sir Cummings'. The superintendent was very impressed when young Tom identified one of the stolen brooches as being for sale in his shop, for a shed-load of money." He knew that would wind him up.

"Oh, he bloody would, wouldn't he. Go on."

"Dora Bream had a ring that was bought from his shop as well. Not that that means much. But we were still checking him out, and tomorrow we were going to search the shop after we got a warrant. Not that we'll need one now. You can't help wondering if this had something to do with the blackmailing."

"I doubt it. We've got that all sewn up, remember. Let's get out of the Crime Scene's way. Not much doubt he was poisoned, though. Make sure you get whatever he was drinking taken away and the glasses he used."

"Beer and brandy. I'll find out which ones. I could smell almonds, so it's more than likely cyanide, Sir. And he dropped like a stone after he had a drink. The landlord was the one that brought him the brandy. And don't forget J. Rich was on that list of Dora's. Do you think we might have been wrong about Major Cove?"

"Absolutely not. Two different MOs for a start. So don't start spreading that anywhere. There's not much I can do here, but I'd better have a word with Rich and his staff before I go. Get the others' details and tell them they can go after you've spoken to them."

Abigail and Terry followed Johnson and Mills out. He stopped to bait Hayley, who was chatting to her husband. He knew she fancied herself as a bit of a medium. What a load of old tosh, he thought.

"Evening, Mrs Bennett. I know you've got special powers, so did you want to tell me whodunnit?" he said sarcastically.

Hayley paused and stared into his red, bloodshot eyes and then said, "Well, I can tell you who's having trouble with his car and who should have some freshly squeezed lemon in warm water for his gout. And who was sitting in a white and red sports car with a well-built chap outside the…."

"Thank you, Mrs Bennett. Lovely to see you again. Why don't you get off home? So get me that list, Tom, and keep up the good work." Mills stifled a laugh. Johnson turned and walked away with a smile turning into a scowl. How did she know his car was playing up and he met up with Doug the Drug for his monthly pay off? Even if she had seen him, how the hell would she know that he had been told yesterday he had gout? He'd make her pay, and that bloody husband of hers!

He found James Rich and Cassie Briggs in the kitchen. Johnson introduced himself and said he needed to talk to the staff and was told it was only them.

James poured himself a scotch and offered one to him.

"I'm on duty, Sir…So make me a coffee and put a large one in it. We'll talk to you first and the lass can wait outside." Once he'd got his drink, he asked the landlord if it was him that gave Banning the brandy.

"Yes, I did, but I didn't put poison in it."

"Was it a new bottle, and if not, when did you last sell a glass?"

"It was already open but was nearly full to the top. I don't sell a lot of it. This is mainly a beer, wine, and sherry pub. I have a feeling I sold one at lunchtime today and the chap didn't drop dead."

"So who could have spiked it? How many staff have been on today?"

"There's only me and Cassie. I had to let my other barmaid go. She was hopeless. These young girls always are. And it can't have been in the barrel of beer as I sold no end tonight. Maybe he'd eaten something earlier."

"Only trouble with that is, if it's what we think it is, he would have died instantly. So you gave him the drink and then what?"

"He put it on the table next to him and I went back behind the bar. There were a lot of people milling about, so I suppose anyone could have slipped something in it."

"We'll have more of an idea when we've checked the bottle, won't we? Do you know anyone who would want him dead?"

"No, I don't. There's a lot more I'd say would be murdered before him in this village. He was a good mate of mine. That's why he helped me out with the quiz tonight."

"Well, that will do for now, Sir. I'll just have a word with Miss Briggs before I call it a night, if you can ask her to come in."

"It's Mrs Briggs, Detective. Can I get you another drink before I go?"

Johnson handed James his cup and saucer. "Yeah, I'll have another one, but this time hold the coffee."

"So your name is Cassie Briggs? How well did you know Julian Banning?"

"As well as I know any of them that drink here, not that well. I run my own cleaning business, so I clean for some of them, but not him. And before you ask, I can't afford to buy anything from his shop."

"But you've worked here long enough to know that he sometimes drinks brandy and what brand he prefers. Did you go near the bottle today, or did you see anyone touching it? Bearing in mind that we will be checking for fingerprints."

"Just because my fingerprints are on it doesn't mean I did it. I can't think when I sold one, but I probably have. I only work here on Saturdays, so I'm not sure if I have touched that bottle or not. Most of the time I'm pulling pints or pouring out wine in this place."

"Did you see anyone go near the glass when it was on the table next to the deceased?"

"Hardly. I was rushed off my feet, so no. I wasn't looking over there. And there were people in the way as well. And I don't know if you know this, but the collection for the charity was on the table as well, so that meant even more people went over there."

"Whose idea was that?"

"I think it was his. I served him his first pint, now I think of it, but I didn't do anything to it, I swear. He had it on the house for doing the quiz."

Johnson scratched his head. "Can you think of anyone that would kill Banning? Anyone he's had an argument with in here?"

"Mmm. Can't think of anyone. He was quite a nice bloke, actually."

"Okay, that will do for now. You can get off home. But you'll have to give a proper statement and sign it tomorrow."

"This is going to be a hard one, Sir," Mills said when she had gone home. "Two murders a stone's throw from each other can't be a coincidence. If it's the same person, it can't be Major Cove."

"Ah, you didn't think of this, did you? Mrs Cove could have done it to make sure we released her husband."

"I didn't see her here."

"Ah," Johnson repeated, "She didn't have to kill him in particular; she could have done it any day. As long as someone died, we would have to think twice about him being the murderer. If I find out she's been here in the last few days, we'll bring her in." He took a last mouthful of scotch and got to his feet. "I'm off home, Sergeant. I'll leave you in charge and expect you to be at the station first thing in the morning with all the information. And make sure that idiot Bennett is there as well."

Hayley had been accompanied back to her house by Terry

and Abigail. Their date would have to wait until another night. Murder came first for The Deadly Detective Agency.

"So are you saying you have been wrong twice in one day?" teased Terry. "The murderer has been murdered."

"So it would seem. What is happening in the world?" Abigail exclaimed. "Is it a blue moon, Hayley? Well, they might need to let Major Cove go now at least. Although Johnson won't want to think they're connected, but they must be, surely. I mean the obvious suspects are James and Cassie. They were both on the list and could have poisoned the brandy."

"But don't forget they both have corroborated alibis for Dora's murder. They were definitely in the pub the whole time, hun," said Hayley.

"Perhaps they did it together. Although, Julian and James are friends. He could have bumped him off anytime when no one was about. You had a good view of Julian, Hayley, did you see anyone go near his drink?"

"I saw Rich take it over and hand it to Julian, and he put it on the table next to his pint of beer. At one point he walked away and talked to somebody, but there were a lot of people milling about going to the bar. And there were others that threw some money in the charity tin. But I can't think of who. The quiz was about to restart so loads of people were going back to their tables. Including Tom and Dave. And I was talking to Isabella so I wasn't really looking. And don't forget there were two annoying spirits I had to keep my eye on. Just in case they got up to no good."

"Who was that then? Surely you don't mean us. I thought we were as good as gold tonight. Was there anyone else there that you knew?" asked Abigail. "You know more people than me in the village?"

"I was really pleased to see Mark Jones had taken his wife to the pub instead of going out without her to the golf club. With a bit of luck he'll treat her better from now on. Oh yes, and that couple that arrived late. I've no idea who they were, not from the village anyway. There was Beverly Hobbs and Shirley Dawkins from church and Miss Spittle from the Post Office and Mr Harding from the charity shop. Cassie's son was talking to his mum at the bar. But he only stayed for about a minute, as she said she was too busy and told him to go home."

Terry said, "It will be interesting to see if it was in the bottle or if someone put it in the glass. They'll probably know by tomorrow."

"Tom said they could tell by the smell and the speed of him dying that it was probably cyanide. Where on earth would anyone have got that from these days?"

"Internet maybe," said Abigail. "You can get most things on there."

"I'm not that convinced about Cassie. I can't get a good read on her. When I asked her round to ask about her doing some cleaning for me, I did feel nervous. She was getting suspicious of all my questions and I got a feeling I shouldn't have invited her into my house. But I'm not sure she's a murderer. But she does have the keys for a lot of the big houses around here, including Cadderly Manor and Dora's, and she would know where all the good stuff was for stealing. And the best way to get in. That reminds me, what did Lillian and Suzie see when they followed her around when she was cleaning?"

"They said she works very hard," said Abigail. "But she snoops. So were they though, I suppose. She looked in drawers and got mail out of opened envelopes that were lying around." Abigail thought that could have been her. She loved a bit of a snoop. "That morning she cleaned for Shirley Dawkins and at the Jones' house. Her son did the gardens at the same time. Now you'll find this interesting, cover your ears, Terry. Rebecca was out there sunbathing in a bikini. So needless to say he didn't get much work done for staring. Let's just say the sunflowers weren't the only thing on stalks."

"In a bikini, wow. She is a beauty," said Terry wistfully. Abigail gave him a 'if looks could kill, if you weren't already dead' look.

"It could be her. She was at the quiz and her husband Mark was on the list, so she could know about the blackmail," said Hayley.

"Very true. See Terry, just because she's slightly attractive, in an obvious kind of way, you can't say she's not the sort to strangle an old woman or poison someone in front of the whole village."

"Why, Abigail Summers, if I didn't know better I'd say you were jealous."

"Don't be ridiculous. Of course I'm not... Well, actually I am, yes. She is gorgeous and alive, but I know I shouldn't resent her for it."

"What would you say if I said you were just as beautiful as her?"

"I'd say you were lying, but what the hell, I'll take it. But I'm keeping her and her husband on the list for now. You look tired, Hayley. Shall we meet back here in the morning?"

"Actually, I can't now. I'm having lunch with Lady Caroline tomorrow and she's invited Fiona Cummings to join us. God knows how I'll bring up the subject of gambling and ask her if she's ever strangled anyone."

"Rather you than me," replied Abigail. "But I'll come with you if you like. Me and Caroline get on like a house on fire."

"That's what I'm worried about. No, I'd rather make a fool of myself on my own, thanks, hun."

"Come to the library straight after then. Right, the others might be annoyed when they realise there's been another murder and we didn't let them know what happened at the pub quiz. It's a shame we were doing so well, weren't we? We'd have won it for sure. Let's get back to the library. Come on, Terry, it wasn't much of a date, but you can at least walk me home."

Chapter 22

HAYLEY DROVE UP THE LONG DRIVE TO CHILTERN Hall in her old red Mini and parked it next to a huge electric car that made it look like a toy. So she reversed it out and parked it on the other side of the steps that led up to the grand entrance. It was a perfect example of Georgian architecture. A young maid dressed in black opened the heavy oak door before she had reached the top. Usually, it was the old housekeeper, Mrs Bittens, who invited guests in. Perhaps she wasn't the only one that wanted to impress Lady Fiona Cummings. Hayley didn't get off to the best start as she realised the large car outside must be hers and she was late. She followed the maid across the spacious hall to the drawing room. Caroline, as usual, was immaculately dressed in cream, and Fiona had that horsey look of tweeds and trousers. She was older than Hayley had imagined and had a pair of metal glasses perched on the end of her nose.

"Fiona, this is a very good friend of mine, Hayley Bennett. But her professional name is Hayley Moon, the famous psychic."

"I've heard of you, of course. You did a talk for us, and I was sorry that I missed it. I was hoping you'd do another one soon."

"I was hoping to myself, thank you."

"I wouldn't miss it either," said Caroline. "Please have a seat. Hayley has the most wonderful stories. She doesn't just hear spirits, she can actually see them."

"That's true. Sometimes a bit too much," Hayley sighed. "But it's usually because they want my help or are trying to tell me something. I have one spirit who is continually asking for my help and turns up at the most awkward moments. But I wouldn't be without her. The other day, I was led by another one to find an elderly gentleman, who was totally confused after his wife passed away. It's hard sometimes, but if I can do some good with it, it's all worthwhile."

"Have you heard of that other marvellous clairvoyant? What was her name now?" said Fiona.

Hayley frowned. "Er, Claire Voyant?"

"Yes, that's the one. I saw she had a large advert in the paper."

"A charlatan, I'm afraid. She was jumping on the bandwagon of other's successes."

"That's right," said Caroline. "It wasn't her that was helping the police. I know that as a fact."

Hayley persisted, "I'm sorry, but I get so annoyed when these fakes try to con people. I dare say she'll make a lot of money from some poor person who wants to talk to their loved one, and will pay an awful lot to do it."

Caroline could sense the anger from Hayley, so she said, "Shall we go into lunch? My cook is away at the moment, so Mrs Bittens did the honours. I'm afraid it's just salad followed by fruit."

Just a salad at the Hall included avocado, smoked salmon, and caviar, so not too bad, thought Hayley. And the fruit dessert was something else - a mixed berry compote. She'd have to do it for Tom; she still had to treat him for the 'him and Mrs Jones' affair. It was four types of berries, mixed with brandy, sugar, and honey and spooned on top of Cornish ice cream. Even she couldn't mess that up.

They retired to the drawing room, as Caroline put it, where the maid brought them their coffee on a silver tray. Lady Caroline fitted perfectly in her role as lady of the manor and poured the coffee like an expert. And surprisingly, she was the one to start the ball rolling about the thefts.

"Did you hear that Fiona and I have both been victims of crime recently, Hayley?"

She had no intention of telling Fiona she was married to a policeman. That had a way of shutting people up who hadn't even got anything to hide. "I overheard someone talking about it in the Post Office. I'm so sorry for you both. Did they get away with much from Cadderly Manor, Fiona?"

"About thirty thousand pounds worth, at least."

"Oh my goodness. You got off lightly then, Caroline, I did hear that you didn't have too much stolen."

"It could have been worse. I will have nightmares from now on, thinking that we were upstairs the whole time."

Fiona put her hand on her heart. "Thank goodness I wasn't home the night that they broke in. I went to the theatre in town and stayed in a hotel."

"What did you see? As you know, I did a bit of acting myself."

"I saw 'The Second Chance'. Ben Callow was very good," said Fiona. Caroline knew Ben very well, and unfortunately for Fiona, she knew that he had left to go back to America five weeks ago. So why was she lying about being there on the night of the robbery? Hayley had already sensed that it was a lie. Fiona had rubbed the side of her nose and looked away.

"Well, at least you will have the insurance money," said Hayley. "That will be a relief."

"Some of the things that were stolen were family heirlooms and irreplaceable. I'm devastated." Hayley did not get the sense that she was devastated. She guessed she had said she was going to London to give herself a reason to be away from the house when it was robbed. But had she killed Dora? And she wasn't at the quiz, so maybe the two murders weren't connected.

Hayley decided to go all in and just come out with it. "I do sense that you are worried about something though, Fiona. It has nothing to do with robberies. Although it could be about money. They say it's at the root of all evil." Oh, no, now Betty's got me at it, she thought. "If you ever want to talk privately and confidentially, I'd be only too pleased to help."

"I can vouch for her. She's helped me in the past, and she's very discreet."

Fiona looked surprised. "Apart from the robbery, I don't think I've ever been so happy." Hayley noticed a slight shaking of the head and a small raising of one shoulder, so she did not believe that for a minute. "I don't know what you're talking about. Edward and I certainly don't have money worries. But if there ever was anything, I would think about consulting you. A reading would be fun, and I could test your abilities."

"Slightly scary, but of course. You have my number, so anytime. I expect you both heard we've had two murders in the village," said Hayley. But surprisingly, neither had heard about Julian's.

"Julian Banning? And he was poisoned? Goodness, what is happening in our lovely village lately? I know him slightly. We've bought a few things from him in the past. And he's appraised a few of our paintings. But who would want to kill him? I know Dora was killed by Major Cove, the Chief Constable informed us," said Fiona.

"Was she a friend of yours?" said Hayley, fishing for answers.

"Oh yes. We'd known each other all our lives and been friends for years. I'll miss her very much." Hayley didn't need to see her touch her nose to know that that was a huge fib.

"They're wondering if the major is guilty now. Apparently, there's a good chance that she was blackmailing half the village, would you believe?"

Fiona didn't answer because she was too busy choking on her coffee!

Terry felt his jaw drop when he saw the newspaper on the stand outside the newsagents. He could see trouble ahead, so he rushed off to find Abigail. They didn't want to tell her, but they knew they had to go and see if Hayley was back from Chiltern Hall yet.

She pulled up in her mini to see the two of them flagging her down outside her house. That was all she needed. Couldn't they give her time to get in the door before they demanded to know how it went at Lady Caroline's?

"Go away. Find someone else to haunt. I'll tell you all about Fiona after I've had a nice cup of chamomile tea, I promise."

"You won't want to miss this," said Abigail. "It's in the local paper and on the news. About your friend, Claire Voyant." That stopped her in her tracks, and so Hayley ran down to the shop and bought herself a copy. She waited until she was sitting in the conservatory before she read it.

The editor had moved the breaking news to the front page. Hayley had a quick scan and told them a condensed version.

"Just listen to this. You won't believe what she's gone and done now. 'Psychic helps police to solve robberies'. Apparently, the paper got a phone call from Claire Voyant who said she had had a vision that she had seen broken glass and a big house had been robbed by a young man. And she saw the letters C and H. Oh right, Chiltern Hall, fancy that. What a phoney."

"She's just guessing, Hayley," said Terry kindly.

"Oh, that's not the worst of it. She says the vision also showed her where he hid the stolen stuff. Honestly, you wouldn't read about it. Well, I have, but you know what I mean. Caroline obviously hasn't been told yet. She would have said. Oh, now she sees the letter U and can hear running water and see a church spire and a grey angel. Abigail, this is your forte, what do you reckon?"

"It's obvious what she means, any idiot could have made that up. But I don't know where. I might if you've got an Ordnance Survey map."

"Um, not on me, no."

"It's in a graveyard, somewhere by a stream or river. Can't be here because there's only a pond, no running water."

"Of course," said Terry. "And next to or under a statue of an angel. How the hell would she know that though?"

"Only one way as far as I'm concerned - she put them there," said Hayley. "It makes me so mad when people get conned like this. If I could get my hands on her, I'd bloody kill her. Hang on a sec, Tom's calling. Hi, hun... Yes, I've read it....Thanks for letting me know.... No, of course, I'm not going to do anything stupid. See you tonight, hun.

Tom said Hudson's boys found the stuff early this morning, in the churchyard at Upper Ansley. There were only two things there, the pistols and the Japanese plate. They must have sold the painting, he says. But if it's her, she must have realised what it was worth and kept it. We've got to find that Claire Voyant quickly. I know, let's go to the paper's head office. With any luck, Celia will be there." Celia Hanson was a deceased journalist who had helped them before. She had an eidetic memory and loved hanging around the paper, where she worked as a crime reporter before she died. Celia had been the main reason that they had investigated the deaths at Gorebridge General Hospital.

Hayley grabbed her keys, and she drove Terry and Abigail into Gorebridge. Hayley waited in the car while they walked, unsighted through the building until they found the well-known journalist.

Abigail saw Celia sitting on the desk of the reporter, Liam, who had taken her job after she had died. As ever, she was immaculately dressed in a tailored suit, her hair cut in a perfect bob. Abigail really wished she had died anywhere instead of in her bed. Then she might be better dressed and not have bed-hair at the back. A bit of make-up would have been nice, as well.

Celia had been keeping a very close eye on Claire Voyant since the story had come out. The only psychic she had faith in was Hayley Moon, as she had seen her abilities with her own eyes. She'd heard the reporter who wrote the story say that he would need an address before they would agree to run it. She was delighted to help them once more and informed them that Claire Voyant was staying at the Grand Hotel, Gorebridge, in room thirty-seven.

Chapter 23

IN ROOM THIRTY-SEVEN AROUND THAT TIME, HUGH was seriously fed up. They had enough for two more nights in this crummy hotel, and that was it. The only phone call they had received was from the Chiltern Weekly, who wanted a follow-up story on how his wife had predicted where the stolen goods would be. And no, there would be no payment, they had said. So they could get lost.

Why did he listen to her? Probably for the same reason all those mugs did. She could talk a nun into having a cigarette and a whisky. So if some poor schmuck did want to talk to his old gran, she'd have him believing she was in the room. She could suss the poor things out in seconds and tell them exactly what they wanted to hear.

Just when he had given up all hope, her mobile rang.

Veronica said, "Wish me luck," and blew out her cheeks. "Yes, speaking... I'll check my diary. Thirty minutes will be fine... The Grand Hotel, Station Road. Yes, Gorebridge. Room thirty-seven. And it's cash only... See you soon... Bye." She threw herself back on the bed. "Oh, my God, that was nerve-wracking. Our first customer, Hugh. I knew as soon as the paper came out and the police found the bag in that church, the phone would ring. Now who's the best con woman in the world?"

"Okay, you are. But all you had to do was sit in the car. I was the one who risked my neck breaking into that house. And do you know how scary that was, going in that graveyard in the middle of the night? I swear to God I heard someone walking about. So don't mess this chance up. Word will soon get around. And make sure you get the money up front."

"I'm not daft. Fifty quid, and I'll ask for another thirty for a palm reading. I've got this. You go down to the bar and give me an hour. I'll text you when I'm done. Give me a kiss. Didn't I say this would work? Right, off you go, I've got to look like Claire Voyant. I wonder what the real one looks like."

Hayley looked red-faced and extremely angry as she parked outside the rundown hotel, but she didn't get out immediately. "What can I say to her? This is a bad idea."

"Why don't you let us come with you? It might get nasty or physical," said Abigail.

"I'll try not to," laughed Hayley. "Although the way I feel at the moment, I can't promise anything, hun."

"I'll come with you then. Not that I can do much," said Terry. "We should have brought Suzie; at least she could have pushed her or hit her with something."

"Don't worry, I'm quite capable of that. I'd rather go on my own. I'll make out I'm a client till I know what kind of person she is, or if she's alone. I'd rather you kept an eye on my car," she said, looking around. "Make sure my wheels are still on by the time I come back."

The Grand Hotel didn't have a foyer so much as a hall, and instead of a lift, there was a narrow staircase with a worn-out carpet. There was a small bar on the left with an assortment of shady-looking customers. She thought she recognised someone and hoped they didn't recognise her. Hayley walked up the stairs to the second floor and followed the corridor to room thirty-seven. She took a deep breath and knocked loudly on the door. It swung back on its own, and she walked in, while calling out hello. Hayley had to stop herself from screaming by holding both hands over her mouth. She often saw the dead in her line of work, but this was the first time she had seen anyone lying face down on the floor, with a knife sticking out of their back.

Hayley felt the woman's wrist for a pulse, but it was too late. She stood up and backed towards the door, unable to take her eyes off the corpse. She knew she should get out her phone and ring for the police, but somehow a stream of thoughts went through her mind. The first one being that Tom might be in trouble. The second one was that Johnson would have her in a cell before she could call a solicitor. She would have the best motive of anyone, and there were now a lot of people who could testify that she was totally loco for talking to herself and hearing voices. She made the decision that hopefully she would be able to work something out before they found the body.

She needed time to think. It was the only way.

She left the door slightly open so someone would at least find the body eventually, while being careful not to leave any prints. She checked to see no one was about and ran back down the stairs. She bumped into a good-looking man at the bottom as he was going up to his room, which unfortunately for her happened to be number thirty-seven.

Abigail didn't say a word when she got back in the car. She gripped the steering wheel and stared straight ahead, ignoring the questions. She started the engine and drove slowly away. She didn't even hear what Abigail and Terry were asking her. They looked at each other and shrugged.

"You don't think she hit her, do you? She was pretty mad," said Terry.

"No way, she's the gentlest soul I know," said Abigail. "I've known her for years."

"She's as white as a ghost. Even whiter than us," he joked.

"She'll tell us when she's ready. Let's give her some peace and quiet until we get back to her place."

Hayley spoke for the first time when she pulled up outside her house. Looking straight ahead and still staring through the windshield, she said, "Go get the others for a meeting. I'm in big trouble."

Within ten minutes, Abigail, Terry, Lillian, and Betty were sitting in Hayley's conservatory. Suzie was sitting cross-legged on the floor, playing with the two cats.

"Come on then, Hayley," asked Lillian. "Did she upset you? What did she say?"

"She didn't say anything. She was already dead. Stabbed in the back." For once, the noisy ghosts were all quiet.

"You poor thing," said Betty. "It must have been an awful shock. But do you think it was wise to run, dear?"

"No. It was stupid. But I think my mind stopped working. I had to get out of there."

Abigail asked, "Did you see anyone?"

"No, but someone saw me. I nearly knocked a bloke flying as I ran down the stairs. I'll have to tell Tom and give myself up."

"Don't be too hasty. Even if the man did see you, it will take a while to find you. Johnson's bound to be given the case. If he knows you were there, he'll have you behind bars before we can work out who did it. He's never arrested the right person yet."

"Abigail's right," said Terry. "He'll have you charged by this time tomorrow. Let's at least think about it. Do you think it's just a random killing, Abi?"

"Too much of a coincidence. It's got to be connected to what happened in Becklesfield. Did you see anything in the room? Any clue at all?"

"Um, it was a bit of a mess in there. I don't think she was the only one staying there. There were a lot of clothes, and now that I think of it, there was a man's jacket hanging on a hook. Maybe a boyfriend or something."

"How old was she?"

"Early thirties, attractive. The door was slightly open, so she must have let him or her in. Maybe even them, I suppose. We need to work it out fast."

Lillian said, "This is DCI Johnson we're talking about. We've got ages before he's even close to making an arrest."

Chapter 24

TOM WAS ONE OF FIVE UNIFORMS TO BE SENT TO THE Grand Hotel, where a body had been found in one of the rooms. He had been looking forward to doing a thorough search of the antique shop, but that would have to wait. This murder didn't have the same appeal. It happened a lot in this part of the town, where the nightlife could get rather dangerous. Although, this lady was killed around three o'clock in the afternoon. He was standing in the entrance, and his job was to stop anyone from leaving or entering.

The bar was already full of drinkers who were all giving their opinions about the murder. "I heard it was a couple that had been here for a week. Bit strange, they said. Good-looking woman, apparently."

"Don't know what they were doing here. Not sightseeing, I know."

"That's true. It was probably the husband who did it. It always is."

"I heard he stabbed her six times. Must have been a crime of passion. There's another man in the mix somewhere."

"Is that right? What do you reckon, Rick? You're very quiet all of a sudden."

Rick took a deep breath. "I'm not getting involved, but I did see a woman go flying out the door. She had long dark hair and a long skirt. Bit hippy-looking, you know the type. I saw her get into a red Mini and roar off. But I'm not making their job easy." Tom's eyes widened, but he somehow kept them looking straight ahead.

In the room upstairs, Johnson and Mills were trying to find clues to who this woman was. The body had been taken, and forensics had finished. They found paperwork that showed she had paid for an advert to advertise the services of Claire Voyant. Johnson would have thought that she would have made more money offering another kind of service in that part of town. Sergeant Mills was searching the room, and DCI Johnson was sitting on the bed. Hugh Stokes was pacing up and down by the door.

"So, your wife's name was Veronica, and you'd been here just over a week."

"Yes, I said. You've got to find out who did this."

"You say she was expecting someone to give a reading to. Man or woman?"

"She didn't say. It was over the phone. She was just so excited. She's so amazing at fortune-telling. I expect you heard she helped your lot."

"You can drop the act now, Sir. And she can't be that good, seeing as what happened here," said Johnson sarcastically. "And you say she was the one who let the police know where to find the stolen goods from Chiltern Hall?"

"Yes. It came to her in a dream."

"Hmm, yeah, of course it did. Do I look like an idiot? Where were you when she was killed?"

"In the bar. When I hadn't heard from her for a good hour and she wasn't answering my texts, I came up."

Mills interrupted his boss. "Sir, look at this." He had opened the suitcase that was in the wardrobe and felt something in the lining."

"Well, I go to sea. Funny how your wife didn't dream that the painting from Chiltern Hall was in your room all the time. Now that is amazing. Did she teleport it here, Sir?"

Hugh couldn't answer that, and if he was honest, he didn't care about anything anymore. He just wanted to know who had killed his beautiful wife. He'd kill them himself when he found out.

"Well, you'll be arrested on suspicion of robbery, but let's get back to the murder for now. Have you any idea who'd want her dead? Was it a widow or widower that she conned out of their life savings, perhaps?"

"No one like that. The phone call today was the first one. Unless you count a lady that lost her dog, and she put the phone down when she found out we would charge her. I can't think of anyone else."

"What happened out of the ordinary? Or did you see anyone come into the hotel when you were downstairs, Sir?"

"People are coming in and out of here all the time. I can't think for shock at the minute. Hang on, I did bump into a woman coming down as I went up. She seemed in a hurry."

"Can you describe her?" asked Sergeant Mills.

"Long dark hair, pretty. Twenties or thirties. Long flowery dress. She had some of those hippy beads around her neck. I remember because they nearly hit me in the eye as she ran past."

DCI Johnson looked at Mills, who had stopped writing in his notebook. "Is that right now, Sir? Would you recognise this woman if you saw her again?"

"Er, yeah, I think so. Do you know who it is?"

"I think I might," said Johnson, smiling, which was very rare. "This could be our lucky day, Sergeant. We'll have this all wrapped up by tomorrow. The murder and the robberies. Well, well, well. Handcuff the man, Sergeant, and read him his rights. One down, one to go."

Hayley got the first text from Tom after they had been home for about an hour. She was pacing the room and still shaking. Luna was rubbing his nose against her legs, hoping for a feed. But for the first time since she'd found him, he had to wait. All the calming techniques she had been teaching for the last ten years were not helping. Why had she run? She didn't know. It must have been shock, she knew that. But would that hold up in a court of law? She looked at her phone and knew it would be Tom. The body must have been found. He was asking if she had been to Gorebridge. She didn't answer, but then he rang her.

"Tell me you haven't been to Gorebridge today, Hayl. A woman's been murdered and a bloke said he saw someone that sounds just like you. She even got in a red Mini."

"Oh, Tom. I went to see that Claire Voyant, but she was already dead, I promise."

"Is that who that is? Oh my God, Hayley. You've even got a motive. They're upstairs interviewing the husband now. I just hope he didn't see you. Maybe Johnson won't find out. I'll do what I can. Gotta go."

Tom put his phone quickly in his pocket, as a beaming and happy Johnson walked down the stairs straight towards him. He knows, thought Tom. He bloody knows.

"So I was sent off duty and told not to take any further part in the case," said Tom. "He can't suspend me because I haven't done anything. And you're innocent until proven guilty. Except in Johnson's eyes, of course. I've never seen him look so pleased with himself. He was rubbing his grubby little hands together, I kid you not. I'll ring the union if he tries anything. I think they'll be able to get me back on the beat, but that's about it."

"I'm so sorry, Tom. I just panicked for a minute when I saw that knife sticking out of her back and all that blood. Then I thought of you and then Johnson. When I read what she said about the robbery, I had to have it out with her. The only way she knew where Lady Caroline's stuff was, was if she took it, and she's my friend."

"More like you saw red that she was pretending to be you. That's what Johnson is going to claim. He'll get a photo off your driving licence and show it to the husband and then check the CCTV for your car. There's a lot of cameras around there for obvious reasons. You're right about them doing the robbery. They found that priceless painting hidden in the lining of their suitcase."

"I knew it. Why did I go? I should have rung you. If only I had left it to the police. I'm so annoyed at myself. What can I do now? I could run."

"Just tell the truth, darling." He sat next to her and took both of her hands. "Anyone who knows you knows you wouldn't hurt a fly." Luna jumped on her lap as she sensed there was something going on. "Or hurt a little pussycat. You saved this little one's life."

She put her head on his shoulder. "But will you still love me when I'm in chokey?"

"What do you think? But it's not going to come to that. Come here, beautiful. I promise I'll be with you all the way. And don't forget that you know some detectives that are pretty damn good. Now, go and freshen up and go and tell Abigail that Johnson is onto you so they can start looking into it. I bet she's in the library. Then I'll drive you to Gorebridge, and we'll find Dave Mills. I'll tell him to ring the Chief Constable to let him know. His wife is a big fan of yours as well, isn't she? Johnson will have to watch what he does then."

"Let's get it over and done with. I know enough to keep these clothes on. At least they won't be able to find any blood splatter. I can't believe I'm about to be arrested for murder. We'll stop at the library on our way. I'll just go and grab some clothes to change into. If Abigail can't help, I've had it. I said that woman held a sword above my head, but I hadn't realised it would be the dagger in her back."

After sitting in the waiting room for three hours, Hayley was at last sitting at a table opposite DCI Johnson and Sergeant Mills. She didn't need a solicitor, he said, as she hadn't been read her rights. It was just a friendly interview at that stage, not that she believed him. Just helping the police with their enquiries, that was all, he had said as they took her clothes away for evidence.

"Hello again, Mrs. Bennett, or can I call you Hayley, or Hayley Moon? I feel I know you, after all, it was only last night that I met you at the scene of another brutal murder. Bit of a coincidence, isn't it? Are you just unlucky, or are you a murderer?"

"Just unlucky, Tony."

"Very, I'd say. So unlucky that I've got enough to arrest you here and now. Me and my sergeant have got you arriving and leaving on CCTV, and a witness can place you on the stairs of the hotel. And now you admit to being in the victim's room. Let's start at the beginning though. You drove to see this Claire Voyant at the hotel. Although we now know her name is Veronica Stokes, a con artist from London. Why did you go and see her, and how did you know where she was? The address wasn't given in the paper."

That was one question she hoped he wouldn't ask her. Tom had said just tell the truth, but that wasn't easy to do. She could hardly say a spirit friend of hers asked a ghost reporter that haunts the Chiltern Weekly. Not unless she wanted to sound like a crazy woman or a liar. "Someone I know on the paper gave me her address. But I can't tell you their name."

"I'm thinking you knew the address because Mrs Stokes had told you over the phone. But we'll come back to that later. So it was a nice friendly chat between colleagues. Not the fact that you were as mad as a wet hen that someone else was taking the credit for your achievements. I find that very hard to believe. Okay, then what?"

"After I was given the address by my friend I drove there and went up to her room."

"And you say she was already dead when you got there? So how did you get in the room?"

"I knocked on the door and it swung open on its own."

"So you admit that you went to room thirty-seven of the Grand Hotel yesterday, to confront Veronica Stokes?"

"Not confront, talk to," said Hayley. "And I didn't know her as Veronica Stokes. I was going to see Claire Voyant, who I knew was a fake medium."

"I expect that's something you would know about, isn't it? Are you sure that you didn't ring her up and make an appointment to have a reading? Because someone did and I'd bet the house on red that it was you. I'll tell you what, if I find the person that gave you the address at the Chiltern Weekly, then I might just believe you. But I'm thinking there is no such person and she was expecting a woman. She had told you where to come and she let you in. And you brought the knife with you and stabbed her. Just because she put your nose out of joint."

"I didn't ring her to make an appointment, you can check my phone. So she didn't tell me where to go. All I wanted to do was to tell her to stop conning people. But it wasn't just that, I thought she had robbed a very close friend of mine, Lady Caroline Hatton of Chiltern Hall. That's the only way she would know where the stolen goods were. I only wanted to talk to her."

"Your close friend, Lady Caroline Hatton of Chiltern Hall, is that right? Name dropping won't help you here, just so you know. The sergeant will tell you, nothing gets up my nose more than someone ..."

"I have got another name to drop for you, detective, just so you know," said Hayley pleasantly. "I think it's Doug." Johnson moved the pages in front of him and looked worried, Mills noticed.

"Doug who?" asked the sergeant.

"I'm not sure of the surname. It will come to me in a minute. Tony might know. He drives a white and red sports car. I think the DCI may have been with him the other night to collect something. Oh sorry, I forgot to ask, how is your gout?"

Johnson cleared his throat. "I think we're getting off the subject a bit, Hayley. And it's getting late. If you write down your statement you can go home when you've signed it. We'll need to speak to you again, so don't go anywhere."

Hayley didn't like to use her powers for evil, but she had to fight fire with fire!

Chapter 25

Hayley was wide awake at five o'clock. She had eventually dropped off to sleep at three. Luna had slept with her all night, sensing that she was unhappy. How did they survive before the little kitten had come into their lives? He always woke her by rubbing his nose on her cheek, but this day she did it to him and lifted him out gently, so she wouldn't wake Tom, then gave him his breakfast and made herself a coffee.

What would Abigail say about the murder? Hopefully not that she was guilty. If she had been thinking straight, she would have rung the police and told her and Terry to go and look round the room. They might have heard the husband say something incriminating, or even the murderer could have still been there. Some detective she was! Shock was a funny thing. Still, no point wishing the clock could go back. As soon as it was open she would go to the library and see if they had any ideas. She just hoped she could get there before she was arrested.

Shortly after nine, Hayley joined her friends, who were so glad to see her. They had all been worried and were delighted that she had been released. They went up to the reference room, where the other readers would not see her talking to herself again.

"So after I played my trump card, he said I could go. My mention of this Doug did the trick, but I don't think it will hold him off forever. It will be my version against the word of a DCI. As I told Johnson at the pub, I saw him as clear as day, being passed an envelope, which you can bet your bottom dollar contained cash. He'll just need a bit of time to cover up what he can. Maybe send this Doug away somewhere abroad. I have a feeling I could be in a cell within a week if we can't figure this out. I might have made things worse for myself, I've made myself a very dangerous enemy."

Lillian reassured her. "No one takes any notice of him. Not even his own men. He might be gone sooner than you think if we can get the major's charges dropped."

Abigail crossed her arms and sighed. "I still think these three murders are connected. The last two are linked by the thefts for sure - that Veronica talking about them to a newspaper and Julian was more than likely receiving stolen goods or even doing them himself."

"There's a word for that," said Betty. "A gate, no a fence."

"That's right," said Lillian. "So who else is on our list? Could you write one for us, Hayley?"

"Yes. It will give me something to do. I think I'm losing my mind. Okay, so at the top shall we put Mark Jones, just so we can eliminate him. He wouldn't want Veronica dead and I can't see him breaking and entering. And I don't think he's capable of murder."

"Although," said Terry, "his wife told Tom that her husband went to Amsterdam a lot. If I remember correctly, it's a well-known place for diamonds and art transactions."

"Well spotted," answered Hayley. "And he was on the blackmail list. So I'll put a star next to him, but I'm really hoping he's not involved, or his wife. Same as Fiona Cummings. She had a motive as Dora had a hold over her at the WI. And she may have pretended to have been burgled when there was a crime spree at other houses. We might not ever find that out, and she'll get a big payout from the insurance. She wasn't at the pub though. Next, I'll add Cassie Briggs. She had an alibi for the first, but could have done the second and the third. If she was involved as she did the cleaning for most of them, then she might think that the Stokes were on to them. Or even raining on their parade by doing a break-in themselves. There's not much honour among thieves."

"And you say I get my sayings wrong," mumbled Betty.

Abigail said, "James Rich is more likely. He was definitely being blackmailed by Dora for being a right pig to women. She must have found out something really serious about him. Perhaps an underage girl or another attack. Can't have been the girl he assaulted in Ridgeway Woods, because the police already knew about that. Julian might have carried on with the threat if he found out what he'd done from Dora. For all we know, he might have found a folder with all the victims' names and the reasons for blackmail in."

Terry agreed. "And then someone totally unrelated killed Veronica Stokes. That could be someone who they had fleeced by saying they were in contact with their dead loved one."

"Apparently though, her husband, Hugh, told them that whoever killed her was the first one who had asked for a reading or anything. One lady had rung about her missing dog but hung up when she was asked for money. He clammed up when they found out that they were both professional con artists. But they worked mainly in London and no one knew they were in Gorebridge. Unless they happened to bump into someone they had conned."

"Marks," said Suzie. "What? I watch TV. Or sometimes they're called gulls. Short for gullible."

"That's very mean," said Betty. "A friend of ours was conned out of thousands. A firm knocked at her door and offered to fix a loose tile on her roof. Before she knew it, they were saying her beams were rotten and she owed them ten thousand pounds for putting it right. She had to pay; she was too scared not to."

"People that prey on the elderly are the lowest of the low. I wouldn't blame them if it was one of their marks who killed her," said Lillian. "Is there anyone else?"

Terry said, "I heard a rumour that Dora had some sort of hold over the Vicar, if you can believe that. It might sound trivial, but he always let her do the flower arrangements or the readings. He could have done something he shouldn't. He's a good-looking bloke and there's a lot of ladies, old and young, that fancy him. And it wouldn't do his career a lot of good if he ministered more comfort to his flock than he should have."

Hayley turned to Terry. "I'll have a word. I'm going to see him anyway to look at the records to see if your birth is written in the parish book. If I'm not locked up, of course. I'll tell him it's an uncle on my mother's side."

"Good idea. Kill two stones with one bush," said Betty.

Abigail sighed again. "I think we were wrong when we said we were wrong. But I might be wrong."

"I think you might have to explain that a bit more, dear," said Betty.

"I'm sure that we were wrong when we said Julian Banning couldn't be a murderer because he was murdered, because I'm sure he murdered Dora."

"You're doing it again, dear. That's as clear as mud."

"I'll start at the beginning. I think Dora sealed her fate when she saw that ring in his shop and asked for money in exchange for her silence. She bought it and then had a hold over him. It also shows that it wasn't just him that did the stealing. If he knew where that ring was from, he wouldn't have had it in the shop and definitely would have snatched it from Dora. He must have bought it off someone unknowingly. But once she told him where it was from, he started his plan. We just need to get the proof and work out how that fits together with the other murders. But it does, I know it does. He wasn't the sort to be bossed around by the likes of Dora."

Hayley said, "So he definitely killed Dora. One down and two to go. Who the hell killed him? And did they kill Veronica? We should see what......"

Just then, Tiggy came racing in through the wall and clawed at Abigail's leg.

"What on earth's wrong, Tiggy? Calm down, sweetheart." She ran off and looked at her and Hayley. "It's like when she wanted me to follow her when I found Luna in the graveyard. Something's happened."

Hayley jumped up and ran out, and Suzie and Abigail went after her. They had trouble keeping up with the ginger cat, but soon realised she was running back to Hayley's house. They all knew Luna was in trouble. By the time Hayley had got her key out to unlock the door, Suzie and Abigail had searched the house, but then they heard a faint meowing coming from the conservatory. Hayley ran in and saw Luna hanging from the top of the Venetian blinds. He had his head stuck between the cords and the slats, so all the pressure was on his thin neck. She stood on a chair and managed to free the kitten, who had gone very still.

Abigail and Suzie looked at each other. Another Luna had appeared, standing next to his mother and looking up at his body. Hayley laid him on her lap and rubbed his chest and blew softly on his nose and mouth.

"Please, God, help this little cat." She kept pressing on his stomach for ten seconds, but it felt much longer. "Come on, Luna, you can do it." They all saw him jerk and open his eyes. Spirit Luna had gone and they all said a silent prayer of thanks.

"Oh my goodness," said Hayley. "Who'd be a mother? That

was the worst moment of my life. Now you're down to seven, Luna."

Suzie picked up Tiggy and kissed her head. "See, your kitten's fine."

"Just in time," said Abigail. "That was a close one. Well done, Tiggy. You saved little Luna again."

"You'd fight tooth and claw for your baby, wouldn't you, sweetie," said Suzie.

Abigail had a thought. Not a major one, but a ghost of an idea. She must remember that pun, she thought. There were a few things that she had to check out. But now wasn't the time. Hayley needed to take Luna to the vet to make sure he was none the worse for his adventure. He had been dead for a few seconds, after all. And she needed to have a word with Lillian; she might know. But first she had to see something for herself. Abigail walked slowly down Church Lane in a very thoughtful mood and made her way to the village green.

Once she had found out what she needed, she sat on her favourite swing in the park. This usually scared anyone who was looking when they saw it moving on its own. Although, hearing about the ex word, she might have to be a bit more careful in the future. According to Terry, a crucifix and a few Hail Marys and she might be sent to Kingdom Come. She wasn't ready for that yet.

This had to be their hardest case so far. There were so many suspects and a lot of them had alibis. But that didn't mean they weren't guilty. She started talking out loud to make it clearer. The only one that could hear her was a small boy at the top of the slide. Abigail stuck her tongue out, much to his amusement.

"Right, so, um, B kills A. Then there's C. Did D kill B? Or was it C or E? I never was very good at algebra. I know one thing, the answer to this is always going to be murder times three." Abigail added an F of her own for good measure!

Chapter 26

LATER THAT DAY, ABIGAIL CALLED FOR ALL MEMBERS of The DDA to meet at Hayley's house. That suited Hayley as the vet had checked over Luna and said he seemed fully recovered from his near-death experience, but should be watched for the next twenty-four hours. Hayley had taken all the blinds down in the conservatory and wouldn't put them back until Luna was much older. She didn't care if it turned into a hothouse. She never wanted to see anything like that ever again. Hayley just hoped they worked out who was guilty before she was arrested. Tom was back at work with Inspector Hudson, working on the robberies, so that made it easier to concentrate on their meeting.

"Now before you say it, Terry, I could be wrong, but I think I know who killed Veronica Stokes," stated Abigail.

"I heard it was a psychic from Becklesfield who killed her," laughed Terry. "She brazenly parked right outside in a bright red car and just walked in."

"Don't even go there, hun. When you put it like that it is a bit worrying."

"Too soon? Sorry, Hayley."

"And I reckon I have worked out who killed Banning."

"I've got faith in you, Abi, and even I have to admit that you're right more times than you're wrong, usually. What was it that tipped you off this time? It's clear as mud to me."

"It was Suzie and Tiggy, believe it or not." She looked down at the ginger cat that was curled up on her lap. "I'll come back to that presently. The catalyst to the whole thing was when Dora saw the ring in Banning's shop by chance. Now the first thing I did after the trouble with poor little Luna was to go to Dora's house. Her two sons were there, but luckily they hadn't moved the two things that I wanted to look at."

"What was that, hun? I haven't got any idea at all."

"A photograph of their wedding and their anniversary. It was a long shot, but Hayley, you know all about fate and destiny, so I had a feeling I'd be able to see what I wanted."

"The ring!" Terry said in triumph.

"Exactly. We needed proof that it was hers or where it had come from. Even that was only a guess on our part. It was on her husband's left hand in the anniversary photo. Now, who had a key to her house to steal it, and used to go there on a Friday when she went to Gorebridge?"

"Cassie. It was her then?" they all said, and added that it made sense as she was on the blackmail list. Although Hayley reminded her about the alibi at the pub which showed she couldn't have killed Dora.

"No, not Cassie." The others all looked at each other. "That's what I thought at first," Abigail glanced at Lillian. "That's until I found out from Lillian that there's another C. Briggs. Cassie's son is called Chris. I didn't put two and two together before."

While everyone was impressed, Hayley screwed up her face. "Sorry, Abi, I had thought of him, but he was checked off the list for Dora's murder. He was in the Dog and Goose in Gorebridge. That would have been too far to get back to Becklesfield."

"I didn't say he killed Dora. But he did break into Major

Cove's house to steal a tie or something to implicate him. Cassie didn't do the cleaning or gardening there. They love gardening and do their own, as you said. He was asked by the murderer, who we know is Banning, to get something. There's no way he would have allowed Dora to live. He told Tom that he'd seen them having words in the past and more than likely he heard what they were arguing about outside his shop. A past affair would be the perfect motive, so Cove would be the perfect patsy."

"Have you got any proof that Chris Briggs took the cravat?" asked Suzie. "I'm dying to know how me and Tiggy helped you to solve it."

"Yes. I'll come to that. It only fits when you've got all the other connections. Banning saw Esme coming out of the gate that night and realised he had the perfect opportunity to use his plan with the cravat. If she wasn't suspected then the major would be. He went home first and then went back later with the cravat. Afterwards, he didn't have time to find the ring or any proof about blackmail, because he knew that Mrs Northover lived opposite and always sat in her window, so he couldn't put the light on. And he knew if he pulled the curtains that would mean that Dora was still alive when Esme left. He must have taken her bag to frame the Coves further, but I'm not sure who actually put it in their bin. It could have been him or the boy. So we were right, we said it was Banning all along, didn't we?"

"But who killed Banning then?" they all wanted to know.

"Now hear me out. Who guessed who it was that was actually doing the robberies? I suspect Dora had first accused her of stealing her husband's ring when she saw it in the antique shop."

"Cassie. Of course," said Betty. "And if she hadn't taken it, there was only one person that had."

"Correct. Do you remember, Betty, when I was killed we had

to think of the motives? You said there was money, love, revenge, and greed."

"Or it could have been...." Terry started.

"Yes, thank you. But thanks to Suzie, I think there's another one in this case - protection. Remember, Suzie, you said how much a mother would do for her child. Fight tooth and claw, you actually said."

"I did, Tiggy saved Luna's life, for sure."

"And who would do anything to save her son? After Cassie was accused, she knew if she hadn't stolen it then her son must have. And once Cassie heard that the major's cravat had been used and he said it must have been stolen the night his wife's jewellery and a bottle of his best whisky had been taken, I think she was sure it was Chris.

No, if she hadn't stolen that ring, then Cassie knew that her son had. No doubt when he was doing the garden he went in Dora's house for the bathroom, or to get a drink. Perhaps she had even seen him drinking an expensive bottle of Scotch. Yes, I know I'm guessing that, Terry.

Plus he worked part-time for Julian at the shop and did their deliveries. Tom saw him there. Chris still lived with his mum, so maybe she had seen him going out the nights of the robberies. She may even have seen Banning's van picking him up outside her house. Burglary was one thing, but making him an accessory to murder was too much. She decided to kill him at the quiz and fight tooth and claw, or rather, nail, to protect her son."

"But Tom said there was no cyanide found on the bottle, and her fingerprints weren't on it or the glass," said Hayley.

"Ah, she didn't need to touch that. She was lucky that he didn't prefer whisky or something like that. A brandy can only go in one sort of glass - a brandy glass. She made sure there were some grains in it all ready for him and put it in the front for Julian to grab. If the glass was upside down as they often are,

I'm sure she could use something to make sure they stayed in. Something see-through and sticky. Even egg white."

"Has anyone ever told you, you seem to know an awful lot about murder?" asked Lillian.

"As a matter of fact my last boyfriend did. He'd got a new car and was showing me, and I just happened to say that it was a lovely big boot and you could get a body in there. Maybe that's why he dumped me, thinking about it.

Where was I? Oh yes, Cassie took a chance that no one else ordered a brandy. But even if they did, she could have picked up another glass. Or if James went to use it for someone else, she could have stopped him and said it was dirty or something. But it worked out beautifully. James said he was going to take Julian a drink and she was laughing. The only time it was worrying for her was when Chris turned up. She couldn't afford for him to be suspected and luckily Hayley heard her send him straight home."

"Truly amazing, Abi," said Terry.

"That's high praise from you."

"Call me old-fashioned," said Betty. "But a judge would say that it's only a guess. What makes you think that he had anything to do with the other burglaries? Pinching a ring from somewhere he works is different from breaking and entering a manor house."

"You're not just a pretty face. Well spotted. I know it's young Christopher Briggs not because he's a thief, but because he's a ruthless killer!"

Chapter 27

"HE'S THE MURDERER?" EXCLAIMED LILLIAN. "IT wasn't his mum then?"

"I'm talking about the murder of that fake, Veronica Stokes. There's no doubt, well not much. I can't think of anyone else it could be. I think it was Chris this time. So Cassie protected him for nothing. I think the stupid boy read about Claire Voyant in the paper and the fact that she said she had seen a young man as the culprit, he assumed she knew something. She even bragged that she could give a detailed description of him. And this was just pure bad luck for Chris, but she told the paper she saw the letter C and the letter H. Obviously, she was making out that it was for Chiltern Hall. But he thought she even knew the start of his name. Murderers, as we found out, are very narcissistic and think everyone is thinking of them. So, of course, if she could see what happened there, then she would know who had robbed Cadderly Manor or the other houses. It's ironic that the only person who believed that she had the gift of second sight killed her. Shows that you should be careful what you wish for. I've got absolutely no proof, though. Although they might be able to trace the phone he used to book the appointment for the reading if they have his number."

"I think I can help, hun," said Hayley, and sat on the edge of her chair. "I saw someone in the entrance to the hotel as I went in and hoped they hadn't recognised me. I didn't know who it was at the time, just that I knew him from somewhere. But now, thinking about it, I know it was Chris Briggs. I'd caught a glimpse of him at the quiz. And if I saw him, then someone else did. I mean, they've got CCTV of my car, so he must be on a camera somewhere. Thank you, Karma. I can't thank you enough, all of you. Johnson is going to be most upset that he isn't getting to lock me up and have Tom sacked. Do you think he'll get the evidence for all the murders, bearing in mind there are one, two, three murderers?"

"Once they know it could be Chris that did the murder at the hotel, I think Tom and Dave will be able to prove it with good old police work. But I have a cunning plan for the other two and it includes taking a leaf out of Dora Bream's book of blackmail for beginners!"

Cassie Briggs heard something come through her letterbox. Her heart lurched as she unfolded it. Someone had cut out letters from a magazine and stuck them down. She read it aloud although she was the only person there. Chris was at the pub again. He always was these days.

"I know your son is guilty of the murders of Julian Banning and Dora Bream. Pay five thousand pounds or else I will call the police. I saw him the night he broke into the major's house. I will contact you tonight."

Cassie poured herself a whisky with a shaking hand. It was too strong and she remembered when Chris had brought it home for her. It was his treat he said and was the best single malt whisky that you could get. Such a lovely boy. She'd give the

The Deadly Pub Quiz

world to have him young again, sitting on the rug, playing with his toy cars. But then she'd heard the major's bottle had been one of the things that were stolen from his house.

If only he hadn't got that job with Banning. He'd been happy being a gardener till then. He thought she didn't know he sneaked out some nights. She had seen Banning's van down the lane, waiting with its lights off. It couldn't have been anything legal that time of night.

The first time she was suspicious of her own son was when she caught him looking through her plastic box where she kept the work keys. Then two weeks ago, Dora had confronted her about her husband's signet ring that she'd just seen for sale in the antique shop. She hadn't even noticed it was missing until then.

That was when Cassie knew for sure. Chris was stealing and working for Banning. So when Dora was murdered, she knew it was him. Yes, Chris hadn't killed her, he was in Gorebridge, but she suspected he had been the one Banning got to steal the cravat. Murder hadn't been on her mind until Dora was killed, but he had gone too far. If she said anything, he could kill her, or even, God forbid, her beautiful, kind son. At the very least, Chris could end up in prison.

Her husband, Darren, had been a professional criminal, and she had tried so hard to keep Chris out of that life. In a chest, up in the loft were all his things that he told her to look after when he ran off to Spain with the rest of his gang. And no doubt there was another woman somewhere. He had shown her what was in there once. There was a gun and some newspaper clippings of heists that he had been involved in. More grisly was a blood-stained pillowcase wrapped around a long knife. And in an envelope, he said was the most deadly weapon of all. Just one grain of the cyanide that was in the vial could kill you stone dead. He'd made a lot of enemies over the years and you never knew when you needed it. Well, she needed it. Their son's life was in danger and she couldn't just stand and watch while he was murdered or sent to jail. But she knew that was her future now. She would miss her house, but not her job.

She had to give herself up, for him. She couldn't let him be blamed for killing Banning, when it was her. She didn't have the money to pay up and that sort never stopped asking for more. Look at Dora. Did she think she didn't know where she got her money from? She knew of at least six other people in the village that Dora had right where she wanted them, even Lady Cummings.

She wouldn't let her own son go down for a murder that she had done, or the one Banning had done. She would have admitted to killing Dora, to save her son even coming into it, but she had an alibi, more's the pity. She couldn't understand who had seen Chris breaking into the major's. He might get a small sentence for robbery and getting the cravat for Banning, but he was an older man and can say he was forced to do it. Her boy was too delicate to kill anyone - whatever his teacher had said. He swore blind to her that he hadn't killed the school guinea pig or that ginger cat a while back, and she believed him.

She might even get an understanding judge and jury herself, who knew she only did it to protect her son from a murderer. She could even get away with it. Then she could keep Chris on the straight and narrow.

Cassie made up her mind and knocked back her whisky and put the glass in the dishwasher. Then she poured the whisky down the sink and put the bottle in a bag to dispose of in a public bin on the way. The blackmailer might keep the information to himself with any luck. She'd get the bus to Gorebridge and give herself up. Hopefully not to that ghastly Johnson. Chris would understand, and he could carry on living here. He'd thank her one day and realise that she had given up her freedom for his. He could have a future now that Banning was dead. She had no regrets for killing the slimy toad. By the time she got out, he

The Deadly Pub Quiz

might have a couple of kids and a lovely wife. He's such a good boy deep down and would make a wonderful father.

Chris was at that moment, having a pint in the Cricketers Inn. He was sitting on a stool at the bar, chatting to the new, very pretty barmaid. He had a smug look on his face. He'd heard that Hayley Bennett was helping the police with their enquiries into the murder at the hotel. What a bit of luck, someone had killed Julian and Dora and now he was off the hook for the psychic woman.

He let out a long sigh, thinking he'd got away with murder. They would never suspect him of being at the hotel. What reason would he have? But he'd heard about a psychic that did a show in the church hall not long ago. Apparently, she'd known everything. Even names and the fact that some woman was pregnant. This Claire Voyant said she'd had a vision of a young man doing a break-in with the letters C and H and even knew where they had hidden the loot. It was on the front page of the paper, so it must be true. If she could see that, what would stop her from knowing who he was. He'd done a lot more robberies and couldn't take the chance that it would lead back to Banning's murder.

Even mum didn't know he had anything to do with them. She'd be mad. If he did anything she'd always say the same thing - you're going to end up just like your father. Well, he'd rather be like him than her. Good job she never guessed it was him that had broken into the Cove's place, to get something for Julian to use. It was either that or the Jones' house, but the gorgeous Becks was always there. Not only that, he would be there for work, so it might lead back to him. It was the perfect frame when Julian told him to put Dora's bag in Grey Towers' bin. Now someone had got him off his back as well. He'd taken all the risks of getting caught in the houses and Julian had made most of the money. He'd keep his nose clean for a while. Maybe even go to Spain to see his dad. His mum couldn't stop him now he was eighteen. She thought he was still her innocent, curly-haired little boy. She didn't know the half of it, he thought. He was a lucky bugger. Yeah, he'd definitely got a guardian angel on his shoulder.

He finished his beer and held up his glass to the young barmaid. He squinted his eyes. As he looked in the mirror behind the bottles, he saw a woman standing behind him. It wasn't a guardian angel.

His blood ran cold and his head buzzed as if it was going to explode. It was a woman he recognised, who was looking into his very soul. The last time he had seen her, he was looking into her eyes and they were in room thirty-seven of the Grand Hotel. She had seen him with the knife in his hand and ran for the bathroom, but wasn't fast enough. So he didn't have to look her in the eye as he plunged the knife in.

He turned around but there was no one there. He must be going crazy. Perhaps it was because he hadn't had anything to eat. He told the barmaid to get him a neat vodka. He downed it in one go and checked behind. Nothing. Just his imagination. Then he slowly turned to look in the mirror. She was still there. Watching and waiting. Veronica Stokes would be there long after the police had arrested him for her murder.

Chapter 28

"NEWSPAPER TIME AGAIN," SHOUTED HAYLEY. SHE HAD found Abigail, Terry, and Betty on the village green. Lillian and Suzie had gone to visit her mother and brother, Jordan. Sonia couldn't see her daughter but felt her presence and it always comforted her, so they tried to go at least once a week.

"Where would we be without the Chiltern Weekly? What does it say?" asked Betty.

"It's on the front page, of course, and they've got photos of Cassie and Chris and a mugshot of the late Veronica Stokes. So the world and its wife know she was a fake."

"She's no Hayley Moon, that's for sure."

"Thanks, Betty. The headline is 'THE MOTHER AND SON MURDERERS - Cassandra and Christopher Briggs.' Basically, it says the mother commits murder to save her son, but it was too late and nothing can save him now. They have both been charged with murder and accessory to murder, for the deaths of Dora Bream, Julian Banning, and Veronica Stokes, by the Gorebridge police. Then Johnson gives a long statement about how he single-handedly worked out the whole complicated case. He doesn't mention he had to release Roland. And not only that, he takes the credit for solving Inspector Hudson's robberies as well. Tom and Dave are not at all pleased, but what can they do? Tom's just happy that I'm not behind bars. He's been worried sick, bless him."

Terry said, "It's not like we can say our ghostly detective agency solved it."

"The only thing Johnson couldn't say was who sent the blackmail letter to Cassie. Hopefully, he'll never find out it was me who sat there for ages, cutting out little pieces of paper. It made a right mess as well. I quite enjoyed being a villain for once. Tom's going to take a week off and we're going to laze about and do nothing. Hopefully with no interruptions," Hayley said, looking at the others with raised eyebrows.

"Scout's honour," said Abigail, with her fingers crossed behind her back.

"And it's no good crossing your fingers, Abi."

"Damn it. I forgot you can see everything," laughed Abigail. "Well, we'll promise to really, really, really try not to disturb you. Unless it's a matter of life and death. You both need a break. But don't forget you did say you would check the books in the church for Terry. But he's waited fifty years, so I don't suppose another week would make a difference. Now, I seem to remember that before all this happened we were going to Chittering Downs for a hike." Terry and Betty reminded her that they weren't going that day. Betty said they were going back to the library for a bit of a break.

"It is called Rest in Peace, you know."

"Very true, Betty. I'll go on my own. I feel like stretching my wings."

"You're an angel as well now, are you?" Terry laughed. "On the other hand, I suppose I could go. I wouldn't want you to be lonely."

"Another date?" asked Abigail.

Abigail and Terry held hands and walked slowly away.

"Another date?" asked Betty. "Have I missed something? Come on, Hayley. You'd better start splitting the beans. I want all the juicy details."

"Okay, Betty, I'll split all the beans."

Terry and Abigail walked up to the highest point of Chittering Downs. There was still a beacon there that had been lit in centuries past, to warn the locals of an enemy approaching. Terry wished he could light it in celebration to let everybody know that he was at last on a date with Abigail and there was no one around to spoil it for once.

"Well, there's no boat or picnic but I've still got the sun and the beautiful girl."

"You old romantic, you. How come you never got married?"

"Just lucky, I guess. No, I'm joking. I'd always had to look after myself since I was young, so I just carried on like that. As I got older, I didn't think I needed anyone. I had friends, just not family. But when it was all over, I noticed people loving and losing and I regretted that I'd missed out. I didn't know then I'd fall for some bossy, big-headed, know-it-all, did I?"

"Oh, really? Who was that?"

"Haha. But she has got another side as well. She'd do anything for anyone. She's very clever, funny, and she can make a ball gown out of an old curtain."

"She sounds like a keeper. I heard she's a good kisser too."

"I'm a detective, you know. So I had better test that theory before I can say it's a fact… Yes, M'lord, I can confirm that Abigail Summers is indeed an excellent kisser."

They lay on their backs and laughed about the shapes that the clouds made as they floated by in the blue sky. Then, just like they had talked about on their dream date, he put his arm around her and they watched the orange sun going down. And this time no one disturbed them.

Chapter 29

WHILE TERRY AND ABIGAIL WERE CLIMBING UP Chittering Downs, Lillian and Suzie were walking across the fields to Little Chortle. They always went together. When Suzie had been knocked down by a drunk driver, Lillian had been at the emergency room of the hospital, as that was where she had died too. The ex-nurse promised to watch over Suzie until her own mother joined her. Jordan, her brother, had taken the death of his little sister hard. Now fourteen, he had studied hard at school, and it was thought to be a certainty that he would go to one of the best universities. Sonia wasn't at home, and Lillian had a feeling that she was in Gorebridge, where she was a social worker. But they should check on Jordan as it was the school holidays.

He wasn't at home either, so they tried the nearby park. Suzie stared at the mothers with their children, thinking back to the time when her own had pushed her on the swing and waited anxiously while she climbed up and went down the slide. How she must have suffered the day that she was run down. Suzie had been in her prettiest dress and was on her way to her best friend's ninth birthday party. Jordan had taken it hard, and his school work had suffered. But now he was the perfect student and had put it behind him.

The council had recently built a basketball net, and they could hear shouting from there. Suzie ran to see what was happening and prayed it wasn't anything to do with her brother. Jordan was surrounded by a group of boys, who looked older than him. They were shoving him around, and one of them kicked him on his shin.

"I'm going to ground you in the dirt, Jordan Marshall."

Suzie shouted, "I'll ground you so far in the dirt, just your head will be showing, you little sh...."

"No, wait, Suzie, he can't hear you," yelled Lillian. "You'll make it worse," and she held her back. "Let's find out where the ringleader lives. It's that big, mouthy one over there."

"You're right." She walked through the others and kicked him behind the knee, and he crumpled on the mud. He had no idea why his leg had given way. But that had given her brother enough time to make a break for it. He ran back to his house and locked the door.

"That will do, Suzie. He's just going to get mad and take it out on Jordan. We'll wait until he's on his own. He won't be so cocky then, trust me. Divide and conquer." Suzie would have loved to just smack him once round the head, but she did what Lillian said.

The five boys shot a few hoops for half an hour, and then Suzie and Lillian followed them as they left the park and learned that the one who kicked Jordan was called Russell. They all seemed anxious to please him, and he knew it. He left his friends and let himself into a terraced house on the edge of the village. He called out in case his mum was home, but the two spirits knew he was on his own, so they smiled at each other. This was going to be fun. It was his turn to be scared and alone.

Russell went into the kitchen and made himself a bowl of cereal and sat at the kitchen table. He shivered and felt a cold draught pass through the room and checked behind him. Suzie looked around and picked up a yellow rubber glove that was on the draining board. She put it on the table with the index finger pointing straight at Russell like a hand. When Russell looked up and saw it, he jumped up and swore. It must have been there before, he thought. He took his bowl into the sitting room to watch some television. He sat down, and his blood ran cold as now the glove was there, pointing at him once more.

This time he dropped his bowl. What was wrong with him? It was just the other glove. The first one would still be on the table out there. But it wasn't. All that was there was sugar that had been spread all over the table. Now he definitely hadn't spilled that.

He slowly crept closer and saw something had been scratched into it. TOUCH JORDAN AGAIN AND YOU ARE... He started to shake and was transfixed with fear as an unseen finger scratched the last word - DEAD. Russell backed out of the room and ran screaming down the street like a baby.

"That was fun, Lillian. Revenge is definitely sweet," said Suzie, pointing at the sugar on the table. Abigail would love that.

"Good one. I reckon that will stop his bullying, but just to be sure we'll come back every day for a week."

"And I'll be there on his first day back at school. Let's face it, all we'll need is a glove. Can we go and check on him now and see if mum's home yet?"

They found Jordan lying on his bed and looking at the red mark on his knee. Suzie laid her hand on it, and the cold immediately made it feel better.

"I wish I could tell him it's going to be alright now. But I guess he'll soon realise. Oh, good, mum's here."

"Jordan," Sonia shouted. "Are you home?"

"Yeah. Up here."

She went into his bedroom and felt her daughter was nearby,

going by the chill in the air, on the warm day. "Everything okay?"

"Yeah, s'pose."

Suzie was surprised. "He's not going to tell her. I would have. The teacher always said to tell someone if you're being bullied."

Lillian replied, "I know, sweetie, but it's different for older kids. But don't worry, we'll be there for him, and I promise I'll let you give anyone a slap if you see it going on. If not, we'll get Hayley and even Abigail on it. And no one will mess with her!"

Sonia could tell Jordan wasn't in the mood for talking. That had been happening a lot lately. "Come down when you're ready, Jordan. I bought some chocolate chip cookies from the bakery."

Lillian and Suzie followed her down the stairs into the kitchen. She sat at the table and put her head in her hands. She wished her son would open up to her. He was twelve when his sister had died, two years ago and, like her, he still wasn't over it.

"Suzie, if you're here, I hope you're alright, but we miss you so much, and I don't know what to do with Jordan. How can I help him to recover from the shock of the accident? He doesn't talk to me anymore." Sonia jumped when a cold hand was laid on her shoulder, but it gave her comfort.

"She's blaming herself for Jordan being upset, thinking it's still about me. She should know about the bullying. I wish we could help her."

"We can, Suzie. Let's ask Hayley to pay her a visit. It's what she does. She'd love to help. Then your mum will find out the truth and might even get closure for herself."

"And I could tell her that I'm fine and I have a wonderful friend called Lillian, who I love very much."

"Bless your heart. Come on, let's go and find Hayley. Jordan is going to be okay, I promise, sweetheart."

Chapter 30

REVEREND PETE HAD BEEN TRYING TO WRITE Sunday's sermon for the best part of an hour. He was bored of it himself, so he knew his congregation would be. He got up and straightened the blinds and then went to make himself a coffee. After leaving it once more to align the ornaments on the mantelpiece, he gave up. His heart wasn't in it and he was just putting off doing it.

So, he was more than happy when he heard the doorbell ring. Any excuse to do it later. He was even more delighted when he saw it was Hayley Bennett.

"This is a pleasant surprise. Come on in. I was so sorry to hear about you being suspected of murder. But I had complete faith that you would be exonerated."

"For a while there, I didn't, but it all worked out in the end. Veronica Stokes wasn't a very nice woman, you know. Neither was Dora actually, it's come to light since. Did you hear she had been blackmailing half the village?"

"I did, and it didn't surprise me one bit. She found something out about my Mary. Nothing illegal, of course, but something private from her youth that she wouldn't want anyone to know. And Dora kept dropping hints to me. I would never have told Mary what she was up to. She would have been devastated, so I did what I could and let her have a bit more leeway with running the church. If it had been anything more, I wouldn't have played along."

Hayley was so pleased to know that the vicar was the good man she thought he was.

"Well, your secret's safe with me, Pete. Actually, it's something totally different I have to ask you. Would I be able to look at the Parish Records? I have a friend of a friend who is trying to trace his family. He thinks he might have been born here in the 1930s. Do you think it might be in the Church Bible?"

"Not in the Bible; that filled up with names in the 1800s, but there is a parish book of births and deaths for that time. It's in the vestry."

"We've been looking for their graves, but we can't see any that we can be sure of. But there may not even be a headstone for them. So many are worn away and unreadable now, aren't they? His father was a local farm labourer, that much we do know."

"There's a book of grave placements as well. They might be in there. I'll fetch the key, and we'll go and look."

"Are you sure you weren't doing anything?"

"Nothing at all," lied the vicar.

They found it in the book of births for the Parish of Becklesfield. Jack Styles and Teresa Styles had a son, Terence William, on February 8th, 1935. But more importantly, Terry had an older brother and a younger sister. Norman was born in 1932, and Vera was born in 1937. Hayley couldn't wait to tell him.

Unfortunately, they also read that Teresa had died not long after Vera was born and that Jack had died two years later. But what had happened to his siblings?

Pete stroked his chin. "There used to be a Norman Styles who came to church here. Unfortunately, I did his cremation service a few years ago. He was a milk farmer, I think. Of course, he was retired when I knew him. But he always had a story about his life. I'm sure he said farming was in his blood. As I remember, he had two daughters and quite a few grandchildren. They live in Chatford, about ten miles from here. I've got their phone numbers somewhere if you'd like them. I'm sure they would love to hear about an uncle. I've no idea where the sister might be."

"I can't wait to tell my friend," said Hayley. "Thank you so much."

"He must be quite an age himself."

"He is. It's almost like Terry is immortal. He's going to be so delighted. He's spent all his life not knowing he had any family. He thought he'd been in an orphanage since he was born. To be honest, it's a modern-day miracle."

"I'm glad to help, Hayley. Tell him to come and see me, and I'll help him find the graves. Now I really must get back; I have a sermon to write."

Reverend Pete said his goodbyes and locked up the vestry. He hurried back to his study to rewrite the sermon. Hayley was right; that really was a miracle. That had given him an idea. He would write a sermon about the greatest miracle he knew, the feeding of the five thousand. But he'd better have something to eat himself first. A tuna sandwich would fit the bill perfectly!

Terry and Abigail were still on their date, so Hayley went home to Tom. She didn't have time to tell him the wonderful news because he said he had a favour to ask. Dave and Isabella had promised to go and visit Mrs Northover. She had been so helpful in Dora's murder and Dave couldn't get it out of his mind how lonely she was. Her son was in Australia, and there was no one else. But then their baby had been unwell, and Isabella said they wouldn't be able to go, as they couldn't risk passing on a cold to the elderly lady. Hayley said she would love to go. She thought of Matthew Rider and how his mind had wandered more as he got left on his own. They stopped at the Village Stores and bought her some chocolates and flowers on the way to Prune Tree Cottage.

"Come in, both of you. That's very kind. How did you know I love chocolates? They'll be gone by tomorrow. I was expecting a sergeant, but a constable will do just as well. And I know who you are. You're Hayley Moon. I heard all about you from my carer. You're that medium who did that marvellous talk for the Women's Institute. I heard it was very good."

"Thank you, Mrs Northover. It did go well. I'll be doing another one soon. Why don't you come? I could pick you up and bring you back."

"That's very kind of you. Can I let you know nearer the time? It all depends on how I'm feeling on any one day."

"I expect you heard that we made an arrest thanks to your help. Your information about Esme's and Dora's movements were so important to closing the case."

"I never thought that Roland Cove had done it. He's a bit pompous, but I could never see him strangling a woman. Now Mr Banning is a different kettle of fish. His dad ran that shop for years and very successful it was too. He looked after his customers, but his son put all the prices up and sold more to day visitors. But of course, when they stopped coming, he'd lost all the villagers. As for Cassie and Christopher, I am very surprised and rather sad. I've seen them both grow up, and I blame Julian and his evil ways. Christopher was such a cute little boy, with his curly hair."

"Is that your son in this photo? He has a lovely family."

"Yes, that's Alex. He went travelling to Australia and married a local girl. They had two children, so it's not as easy for him to come and see me. But they're nearly adults themselves. It's my fault; I should have visited them when I was younger. I don't think anyone would insure me now, and it's much too far for these old bones."

"Never say never," said Tom. "Have you always lived in Becklesfield?"

"As far as I know, I'll tell you a secret. I found out when my mother died that I was adopted. My father could finally tell me. She'd never wanted me to know in case I thought differently about her. Of course, I never would have. I loved my parents dearly. I was in my fifties by then, so it was a bit late to do anything about it. I found out they adopted me when I was two years old. They couldn't have children, so I was an only child and I had a lovely childhood. I was their life, you see."

"Do you know anything about your real parents?" Tom asked.

"Not an awful lot. My mother died not long after I was born. It was during the war, so hard at the best of times. I was told my father was a farm labourer around here somewhere. He wasn't called up to fight as farm workers were a reserved occupation. Keeping the country fed was as important as being on the front line. And they had to fight the fires caused by the bombs at night. I think he was finding it hard to cope. Well, he died not long after his wife, and luckily I was given a home by two wonderful people."

Hayley felt a tingle spread over her body. "I don't suppose you know your original surname, do you?"

"Yes. My father did tell me that. It was Styles."

"Mrs Northover, by any chance, is your name Vera?"

"It is. How clever of you. I'm usually just Mrs Northover now. All my close friends have passed as well. However did you know that?"

"It must be a day for miracles. Reverend Stevens helped me to look in the parish records; it wasn't just you on the farm when your parents died, you had two brothers, Terry and Norman."

"Oh my goodness. I always had a feeling that something was missing as I grew older. Almost like you would if a twin went missing." She took out a linen handkerchief from the sleeve of her silk blouse and blew her nose. "I'm quite overwhelmed, dear."

"I'm so sorry to spring this on you. It must be a shock. But I should also say that they have both passed."

"I see. I thought perhaps they had. Can you tell me about them though, please?"

"You had a younger brother called Terry. He wasn't as lucky as you, and he was put into an orphanage." Lisa shook her head and wiped her eyes. Maybe this wasn't a good idea, Hayley thought. "Don't worry though, he had a lovely life. But we'll come back to him. I'm not sure what happened to Norman, but he had a good life as well and the exciting thing about him is that he had two daughters and grandchildren. They live not far from here and the vicar thinks they would be absolutely delighted to know they have an auntie. This is a good thing, Vera. You have a family now. You'll have people that love you again."

Vera leaned back in her chair and closed her eyes. Tom and Hayley looked at each other, worried that the shock had finished her off for a minute. But she opened her eyes and said, "Thank you both so much. The hole I have felt all my life has finally been filled. Thank you. But how did you know all about them and connect it with me?"

"It's quite simple, actually. You know what I do, Vera? You know I'm a spiritualist. Well, I am in frequent contact with Terry. He didn't have a clue that he had a family either. It wasn't until he went to a tied cottage for farmers and he had a feeling, a bit like yourself, that he had been there before. Then he knew he had to have lived somewhere other than the orphanage.

He contacted me, and I have literally just found the entries of the births in the church records. The fact that we came here today I think can be put down to a power far greater than mine."

"That is so true, Hayley. Do you think I could connect with Terry one day?"

"That is a definite, Vera. He doesn't know anything about this yet, but I don't think I could stop him if I tried," she laughed. Hayley knelt down next to her and gave her a hug. "I've got your nieces' phone numbers, and I'll tell them the good news tomorrow. I don't normally give fortunes, but I have a vision as clear as day, that Alex will come here with his family and will be meeting his cousins. Just when we think we've seen it all, life always has a way of surprising us, doesn't it?"

Hayley went and put the kettle on and made them all a cup of tea. She even put Vera's in her bone china cup and saucer and not a mug. The box of chocolates stayed unopened next to her chair. She was going to be forever grateful for Hayley's news, but she planned on having them all to herself later. Some things were just sacrosanct!

Terry walked with his arm tightly around Abigail as they walked back down the hill to the Becklesfield Public Library. The full moon was high in the sky as if Terry had arranged it for their perfect date. He was still on cloud nine and thought this was the best day of his life and death. He was oblivious to the wonderful news that Hayley would be giving him in the morning.

"I wonder what the time is?" asked Abigail. Terry was going to be brought back down to earth with a bang. "Sorry, didn't I tell you? The Deadly Detective Agency has got a customer booked in at midnight. It's a lady who thinks she must have tripped and hit her head and died. But somehow we have to tell her that there's a knitting needle sticking out the back of her neck. We'd better find the others; it's going to be an exciting night!"

Chapter 31

AN ATTRACTIVE WOMAN, SMARTLY DRESSED IN A DARK blue jumper and black trousers, entered the library at exactly midnight. Their new client, Hannah Clark, was introduced by Abigail to Terry, Betty, Lillian, and Suzie, and she sat down opposite them in the library.

"I don't know what I'm doing here, if I'm honest. I had never heard of you until yesterday. I just knew I had to come. But I'm hoping you can help me. I seem to be in a bit of a daze."

"Can you tell us a bit about yourself before we start?"

"I'm thirty-three, married, with no kids, and I work part-time at Paxtons, the men's outfitters in Gorebridge. My husband runs a building business. Why I'm dead, I have no idea. I think I must have fallen and hit my head, that's about it."

"Believe me, I know what you're going through," said Abigail. "I was totally confused. What happened? Can you tell us what you know?"

"I was getting ready to go to Crafts and Laughs at the village hall. It's run by the church. After Christmas we start making things to sell at the Autumn Fair. It's a bit of a social gathering as well. It's always the last Thursday of the month. It's in Little

Frimble where I live, not in Becklesfield. I'm not sure how I even got here. So I can remember walking in the door and sitting and doing some crocheting at our table. Lisa was showing everyone a new stitch that she had just learned. She's usually in charge of the knitting but we wanted to do something else for a change. We've been making hats for premature babies at Gorebridge Maternity Hospital. But that's by the by. We've actually made twenty-nine so far," Hannah said proudly.

Betty started talking about baby hats and how many she had made over the years, so Abigail hurriedly got her back to discussing the investigation.

"Tania was in charge of the other table. They were cutting out cardboard bookmarks and painting them. Then I can remember Pat, the caretaker, making the tea and joining in making the bookmarks with Tania. There's usually about ten people there, but that day there were only seven of us for Crafts and Laughs."

"And was it?" asked Lillian. "Crafts and laughs?"

"As a matter of fact, that day it wasn't. There was an awful atmosphere. It started when Lisa was showing off her hand-knitted, navy jumper she was wearing. It had cable at the front and plain stitching at the back, as Tania pointed out. There were a lot of snipes between them. Then when Tania said she was making bookmarks, Lisa muttered that it was a wonder she had time to read. So I don't know what she meant by that. And when Lisa said she was going to teach them how to do the diamond crochet stitch, Tania mumbled she'd never get a real one and was good at getting her hooks into people. I have no idea what was going on between them. Neither are married. I mean ladies aren't in as much hurry these days, are they? I got married at eighteen and had fifteen years of wedded bliss. Well, for the first five years anyway. I wonder if he'll remarry now."

"All that sniping must have been very awkward for all the rest of you," said Betty.

"Very, but we loved it! Lots of nudging and sniggering. Much better than knitting and making small talk. They should have called it Stitching and Bitching; they would have had a lot more members." Abigail reckoned she would have enjoyed that. Far better than the tap and line-dancing in their village hall that she had done for one session each. "Anyway, after the others went, me, Lisa and Tania cleared away as we always did."

"Sounds to me like there's a man at the root of this," said Abigail. "Any idea who it could be?"

"I haven't a clue," said Hannah. "If anyone knows, Pat will. Us four were very good friends. We always went to the pub after every Crafts and Laughs."

"The caretaker? Where can we find her? Does she live in Little Frimble?"

Hannah laughed. "Pat is a him. And an extremely good-looking one!"

"That makes all the difference. 'Cherchez l'homme', as they say. What was he doing while all the bickering was going on?" asked Abigail.

"Pat, Patrick was there, so he must have heard some of it. He was in the kitchen or helping with the bookmarks mainly. He definitely never knitted or crocheted. We had a cup of tea, which tasted dreadful as usual and after the others had gone, us four tidied up. We swept up all the bits of wool and paper and put the tables and chairs back against the wall and Pat washed up the tea things."

Betty wanted to know something about the other three.

"I like Lisa. She's a lot of fun. Very outgoing and always has a boyfriend on the go. She used to go out with my husband before I did, but that didn't matter to either of us. She could be a bit selfish at times. She's an author and writes very steamy mystery stories. 'Tied and Died' is her best-seller. Have you heard of it?" asked Hannah.

"No," said Betty, "But I'm sure going to find it if I can.

Sounds good. As I was telling the others, me and my husband, John, used to..."

"What can you tell us about Tania?" asked Abigail quickly.

"She's a lot quieter. She's an artist who has a studio built onto her house. Gets paid a few hundred per painting. Never married and as I said before, she clashed with Lisa sometimes. Pat was single too, but never short of female company. He did a lot for the church and he was a sucker for a good cause. Pat was some kind of financial advisor and worked from home, so he could choose his own hours."

"Do you think there could have been a love triangle between them?"

"Hmm. It sounds like it, doesn't it? I didn't think so at the time. But looking back I have a feeling that he was keen on Tania. They always seemed close. After the pub, they would walk home one way and Lisa and I would walk the other way. But I can't remember leaving the hall that day at all, let alone reaching the pub. Why can't I?"

"Abigail will work it out," said Terry. "She's got a very sharp mind. Why did you think that you had fallen and banged your head?"

"The ground was slippery that day. It was just a process of elimination really. What else could it have been?"

"Why was it slippery? Had it been raining?" asked Abigail.

"Not that I can remember."

"Ah," started Abigail. "Prepare yourself for a bit of a shock, Hannah. The first thing is that I don't think that you have died in the last few days. Paxtons, where you worked, went bankrupt in March. I can't think why Lisa would have been wearing a cable jumper as it's August and definitely not cold or slippery. So it must have been months ago. And the other thing we have to let you know is that you definitely didn't slip!"

Chapter 32

SO MUCH FOR HER WEEK OFF, THOUGHT HAYLEY. Luckily Tom had gone to visit a friend in London, so he had not been there to see Abigail, Terry and Suzie burst in. Hayley thought she had the house to herself, so she had booked in a reading with a new client.

It wasn't going particularly well. Roger Hardy wanted her to get in touch with his mother-in-law, to tell him where she had hidden her jewellery before she died. Not for love. No wonder the lady in question hadn't appeared. They both felt the drop in temperature as her friends arrived. Hayley didn't like to tell him that it was someone for her and not him. They started telling her about someone called Hannah. When she told them to be quiet, Roger thought she was talking to him and called her a fraud.

"No, not you. I'm talking to a spirit. No, sorry, it's not your mother-in-law, so I can't tell you where the jewellery is."

Abigail got close to her ear. "Tell him you'll try and make contact tonight and find out. In the meantime Suzie and I will go round there. To prove your powers, tell him to keep his eye on…er, that angel ornament. Go on, Suzie, do your thing."

After the angel had flown through the air and landed gently on his lap, he thanked her quickly and ran out the door, telling her to ring him.

They all started laughing. "Another satisfied customer, eh, Hayley?"

"He was awful. But if you could go round to Mrs Goggins' house I would appreciate it. But I think I'll tell his wife where the jewellery is, not him. Now what can I do for you guys?"

"We need to get hold of Celia Hanson," said Terry. "And we're in a bit of a hurry. We can't use the library to look at the old newspapers because Janette, the librarian is on and we've already nearly given her a heart attack moving things around. But Celia has a photographic memory and she'd already know exactly what we want. She's like an encyclopedia of suspicious deaths in the county."

"And you expect me to give up my precious time off and drive all the way to the Chiltern Weekly offices and see if she's there, just for an investigation?"

"Yes."

"Try and stop me," laughed Hayley. "But first, I have something to tell you, Terry. You better brace yourself and sit down, hun. And I have to warn you, it's good news and good news!"

Celia wasn't very hard to find. She was sitting in the entrance of the newspaper office where she had worked. Death could be very boring when you'd had a busy life. She was delighted when she saw Hayley arrive outside in the red Mini and noticed Abigail in the passenger seat next to her. She fancied a drive out into the countryside and half an hour later, they were sitting in Hayley's sitting room. The last time they had all been there was when Abigail had brilliantly worked out who the serial killer at the hospital was. Celia had been telling her editor for months there was one, but no one believed her until Hayley, Abigail, and the rest of the famous paranormal detective agency helped her to prove it. At that time, she was one of their first clients.

"We're a bit pushed for time on this one, Celia. We can't look at the archives in the library because Janette, the librarian, will think she's being haunted again. You see, we had a lady called Hannah come to the library last night, who was very confused and it was death by knitting needle."

"I think I know the case; there's not too many killed like that." Abigail went on to tell her how she was at her craft club and the suspects were Tania, Lisa, and Pat because Hannah could remember everyone else leaving.

"Now, seeing as you have an eidetic memory, we are hoping you can recall all about her death. I know you like the inquests of murder victims."

"I do indeed. What's her full name and when did she die?"

"Hannah Clark, and I think she died about six months ago. Oh, and it was in Little Frimble."

Celia looked upwards for a few seconds and then nodded her head. "Hannah Clark. Age 33. Married. Died thirteenth of February. Unlawful killing."

"Amazing, hun," said Hayley. "Now we've got to work out who did it out of the three."

"No need for that," added Celia. "I hate to tell you when you're on the hunt, but they know who did it." Celia looked up again. "Lisa Taylor. Author. Age 35. Also died on the thirteenth of February. Suicide."

"You're kidding," said Abigail, disappointedly. She nearly swore for a minute.

"Nope. They found a suicide note admitting to it. Well, it said, 'I'm so sorry, Hannah. I shouldn't have done it.'"

"But that could mean anything. Sorry I scratched your car, or pinched some flowers from your garden. Or had an affair with your husband. I don't suppose it was dated either. No, I didn't think so. Seriously, what investigator in his right mind would close the case on that flimsy evidence?"

"I bet you can guess. Your friend Detective Chief Inspector Johnson."

"I might have known. Was there any more proof?" asked Hayley.

"Only that her fingerprints were on the knitting needle, but she did most of the knitting there, so it wasn't surprising. She went out with Hannah's husband once, so her friends thought it might have had something to do with that. Her body was found next to her mother's grave and she had overdosed on sleeping pills that had been prescribed for her. So it was pretty damning."

"That reminds me, Hannah said the tea tasted awful. Supposing the tablets were in that. They would both have been easy to kill. It can't be Lisa. There's a reason why Hannah came to us now, six months after it happened. She would be resting in peace if she'd had closure. Let me think for a minute."

Abigail leaned back in the chair and closed her eyes. After a while, she started moving her hands as if she were moving imaginary chess pieces. Hayley and Celia had seen this on other cases. Just before she had a brilliant epiphany and cracked the case.

"Now, this is a real stab in the dark. Ooh, I like that one. I'll have to tell Terry. Now, Celia, I know you always read the Chiltern Weekly, so you'll know this. I read it myself when we were investigating our last case. It was one of the things Dora Bream had been reading and might have been going to cut out. Little Frimble rings a bell. Do you remember, of course you do, reading that someone local had won the lottery?"

Celia thought for a second. "I do, but that was a man. His name was Patrick Bates. Oh. I see, Pat. Lived in Little Frimble and he won a rollover - eleven million."

"Just as I hoped. I think they had a syndicate. It was Thursday, the day after the draw. Hannah and Lisa didn't have a clue that they had won."

"But Patrick had an alibi for the murder. He was with Tania, in the kitchen. They heard a crash and Hannah was lying face-down on the floor with a knitting needle in her neck and Lisa was missing," said Celia, as she recalled what was written in the paper at the time. "They found her at ten-thirty that night in the churchyard."

"This is what I'm thinking, Tania and Patrick were in it together. They could alibi each other so why share the eleven million if they didn't have to? They drugged them both with the tea and then stabbed Hannah, after making sure Lisa's were the only prints on the knitting needle, and then hid her drugged, unconscious body somewhere close by and called the police. He couldn't have done it on his own. Then they fed her more tablets and left the body and the note in the churchyard. Maybe they forced her to write the suicide note. I expect even Johnson would check it was her writing and only her fingerprints."

"I think you're right, hun. But what made you connect the deaths with the lottery win?"

"I believe in karma as much as you, Hayl. There must be a reason that Hannah was compelled to see us. The six or seven months had to mean something. I tried to think if I could remember anything that happened in Little Frimble when I was alive, but I thought I'd read something last week. Now before I get too excited, Celia, how long do you have to claim a lottery win?"

"Hmm, one hundred and eighty days, around six months or else it's invalid."

"They wanted to leave it as long as possible. Even Johnson would have seen a huge lottery win as a big red flag. Now, I know you're on holiday, Hayley, but shall we go to Little Frimble to see what's happening in the lives of the new millionaires? That is if they haven't run off to Panama or somewhere."

"Let me think about it. I've thought about it. Let's go!"

Chapter 33

HAYLEY FOUND OUT THE ADDRESSES AND THEY WENT to Patrick's house first. It was a big, detached house with a double garage. It was locked up tight and there was a 'For Sale' sign outside. Celia and Abigail tried to look in the windows and then realised they could walk in anyway. The place looked a total mess. Patrick had obviously left in a hurry. Hayley caught the neighbour's eye as she was leaving her house.

"Excuse me. Have you seen Patrick Bates? I was hoping to have a word with him."

"You and a lot more besides. He packed one suitcase and left the day after his big win last week. I suppose you can buy new when you've got eleven million in the bank. And no, he didn't give us anything, not even a goodbye. We'd lived next door to him for twelve years and not so much as a thank you for all you've done."

"Do you have any idea where he went?"

"No. He just got in his car and drove off."

"Was he on his own?"

"As far as I could tell. He did have a lot of female company, but not on that day. He might have picked someone up though."

"Well, thank you for your help, and I expect your new neighbours will be a lovely young couple."

They didn't think Tania would be there either but had to make sure, so they were surprised when there was a light on in the terraced house where she lived. They knocked at the door, which was answered by a scruffy-looking woman. She, in turn, looked at Hayley and wondered what she wanted. "I don't want anything and I haven't got anything, so get lost."

Hayley felt this woman is in a lot of pain. This woman needs me. She sounded drunk and was unsteady on her feet. Either that or she was on strong medication.

"Tania? I think you had better let me in. My name is Hayley Moon and I've been talking to Hannah."

Tania stumbled back and said, "She's dead."

"Nevertheless."

"You'd better come in," said Tania, and walked slowly into the kitchen while holding onto the wall for support. Celia and Abigail followed in Hayley's shadow, unseen. She picked up a dirty glass that was stained with red wine and took a large mouthful.

"I know this is a shock for you, but I'm a medium and Hannah has asked for my help to rest in peace. I know everything. What you did to Lisa as well."

"Nothing to do with me," she slurred. "Ask him."

"If you mean Patrick Bates, we tried but he's gone."

Tania started to sob. "You don't have to tell me that. He told me he loved me and we could start a new life abroad. He told me about Thailand and how it had always been his dream to live there. It was all his idea. The only thing I did was help to lift poor Lisa. She was my friend. I just got caught up in it. He didn't give me the chance to think. I loved him and just thought of our future together. He said we couldn't be seen together until he had been given the cheque, and then he'd move the cash abroad and we'd leave for Bali, or somewhere exotic, and live in luxury for the rest of our lives." She wiped her eyes and nose on her sleeve.

"When did you realise?" asked Hayley.

"The day after he got the money. I went round to his house and he was throwing out stuff. I told him I was ready to go and how much I loved him and he wouldn't need to pack much because we could buy new when we got there. That's when he said he was going on his own." Tania's voice broke and the tears rolled down her cheeks. "The money was in his name and he never intended sharing it with anyone he said. Us four had been doing the lottery for months and as the time went on we stopped checking. He told us that he always did. He let us know when we won thirty pounds and so we believed him.

After they found Lisa's body, he told me to start a rumour about her and Hannah's husband. They were old friends and luckily for him, he had an alibi. He denied it, of course. The talk got so bad that he had to close his building business and move up north. I think Patrick bewitched me. He only had to ask me to do something and I did. What a fool. The last six months he said it was too suspicious to be seen with me, so we only met up a few times. We needed to leave it long enough that no one suspected, and then he would make out he had just checked the winning numbers. He never made love to me after either. But he still had me hanging on a thread. I was wishing the days away till we could get on that plane. I can see it so clearly now. I deserve everything I get.

That day at his house, he told me he had never loved me and had used me from the start. It was only that I was the most gullible and stupid out of the three of us women. He said he could have chosen any of us. Patrick knew I couldn't go to the police without ending up in prison for the rest of my life. I've thought since it might be worth it to see him in handcuffs. But he's gone. I doubt they could find him if they tried. He could be anywhere in the world. And I'm stuck here with all the guilt for what I've done. That will stay with me till the day I die. I only hope that's not too long. But I'm frightened of that as well."

"I'm so sorry. You were used, Tania. He manipulated you, using love, and his only thought was greed."

"I suppose you'll have me arrested now, won't you? I don't care either way," she shrugged and took another mouthful of her wine.

"I don't have a choice now you've told me. I have to get justice for Hannah and would be an accessory to murder if I looked the other way. I'm so sorry. It would look better if you handed yourself in. I know a sergeant in the CID; he'd be very gentle with you."

"I haven't finished one painting since the day they died. All I can see on the canvas is their faces looking at me. My brush seems to take on a life of its own and before I know it, there they are. So I'm not even surprised Hannah is still here. So I'll do it. I'll miss my garden, that's all. Okay, let's get it over with. I knew this day would come sooner or later. I'll tell the police everything, I promise. I don't even know who you are." Tania smoothed her hair down and walked slowly to the front door in front of Hayley.

"I can't do it, Abi," she whispered.

"I was going to say the same thing."

"The evidence wouldn't be admissible in a court of law," Celia added.

"Wait up a minute, Tania. Let me think. We're not, I mean I'm not with the police, so I don't see why you should suffer while that man has got away with it. It sounds like you've been through enough and he did the actual murders. Justice would serve no purpose in this case. I'd like to think that you'll still have a life, especially if you stop drinking. And you do sound genuinely repentant for what you've done. Perhaps you could see a doctor and get some help. I can't let him ruin all your lives."

"Do you think Hannah and Lisa would understand and forgive me? I am so sorry and ashamed."

"I'd like to think they will. They will know that you're a victim as much as them. And don't worry about Patrick Bates. I always believe in karma, so I wouldn't be at all surprised if he got his comeuppance as well. 'The evil of man is followed by neither angels nor good fortune'."

Philip Booth looked at his brand new passport. He had kept the initials the same as Patrick Bates to help him remember. He'd paid a lot of money in Mexico to get a complete set of papers in his new identity. But what the hell, he still had millions left. He'd put all his lottery winnings in an offshore bank account in his fictitious name. That had taken four months to get going. A contact in London had given him the address of the Castillo brothers, who could get him what he needed once he got there. Expensive, but top-notch. And cash only. He had taken out enough to fill a suitcase at el banco in the town, so he could go off the grid for a couple of months. He'd been careful that no one saw him when he took the pesos out to pay the pair of them. They wouldn't have said anything anyway. He'd paid them enough to buy their silence.

First thing he had to do was get a car and then he'd have a drive down the coast to find a villa. Nothing too extravagant. Maybe a small pool, though. He was already sweating in the humid heat. A pool was always good for the ladies, and he wanted to meet muchas ladies. How Tania could have thought he wanted to spend the rest of his life with her, he couldn't imagine. He just hoped she'd keep everything to herself. She had more than him to lose. Just as well he didn't tell her where he was going, though. He'd mentioned Thailand, in case she had a sudden desire to get it off her chest, for guilt or more likely revenge.

The two men who had sold him his passport had given him the name and address of a friend who could sort him out some wheels. He made sure to say he didn't want a stolen car, or anything too flashy. It all had to be legit. Where was the damn place? He had left behind the row of small shops and was heading towards a residential area. Not that he would have wanted to live there. It was starting to look a bit rough, but he could take care of himself. The houses he passed now had scaffolding and looked more like derelict building sites. The further he walked, the fewer people there were. He did start to worry when he came to a dead end without seeing any sign of cars for sale. He held a tighter grip on the handle of the suitcase, conscious of what it would mean if anyone got hold of it.

Patrick Bates, aka Philip Booth, never even heard them coming, as Juan and Jose Castillo crept up behind him and shot him twice in the head. Karma had decreed there should be one bullet for each woman's murder.

Chapter 34

IT WAS THREE WEEKS TO THE DAY SINCE DORA BREAM had been found dead. Today, Shirley Dawkins had arranged the flowers for the church service, and Beverly Hobbs had delivered the reading. Esme arrived at the church with her husband for the first time since his release, to be greeted with smiles and handshakes. Peace, harmony, and tranquillity had once again been restored in Becklesfield.

Hayley met Abigail, Betty, and Terry for a Sunday afternoon walk through Ridgeway Woods. He was still disagreeing about letting Tania go free.

"She was there when he killed two of her friends and did nothing about it. If it weren't for the fact that her partner in crime was so despicable, she'd be sitting under a palm tree herself."

"I wish I was," said Betty. "The nearest I got was under the pier in Brighton."

"Me too. I'd say it's never too late, but it probably is in our case," said Abigail.

"Anyway, Terry," said Hayley, "Hannah was our client, and she wanted to give Tania a break. Enough lives have been ruined. She agrees with me that Patrick will face his own punishment one way or another."

Abigail added, "Apart from what Tania told us, I doubt there's any physical evidence after all this time. Maybe they could exhume Hannah's body to see if she had been given sleeping pills, but she wouldn't want her family to go through that and then possibly a court case and all the publicity. They're just beginning to come to terms with her being murdered. We'd only be doing it for vengeance."

"Can you imagine what Johnson would say, hun, if we said he was wrong again? It would almost be worth it to see his face. And if he had done his job properly in the first place, Patrick and Tania would be locked up now. Sorry, Terry, I think you're outnumbered on this one. Hannah hasn't forgiven Tania, nor should we, but sometimes we need to let that person out of our heads, for our own well-being. Not forgive, but try to forget if we can. Tania will never forgive herself for what she did to Hannah and Lisa, and that should be enough for us, hun. Especially in our line of work. If I held everyone's troubles in my mind and heart, I'd have no room for the wonderful things that happen in my life and the miracles I've seen. Then I'd never be able to help the next person."

"I'm sorry, I see that now," he said. "Onwards and upwards."

"Thanks, hun. But before I forget, they've taken James Rich in for questioning. The barmaid you told us about, who slapped him, and at least five others have come forward to say they had been assaulted by him. They're sure to reopen the case of the girl he gave a lift home to as well."

"Another success for The Deadly Detective Agency. I just wish we could get the acknowledgement sometimes. We could do with someone writing our cases in a book like Dr Watson, or should I say like Conan Doyle did for Sherlock Holmes. Do you know anyone who could do that, Hayley? It could be called The Casebook of the Deadly Detective Agency. Or the Abigail

Summers Mysteries. Not that I'm one to sing my own praises, as you know," said Abigail.

They all laughed together. "Oh my God, Abigail. You sing more than a choir at Christmas," said Terry.

"Charming. Well, if I don't toot my own horn, no one else will. So much for my friends," laughed Abigail.

"I might actually know someone," said Hayley. "I could have a go. I was good at English at school. I'm sure I could write the individual cases down as we solve them. It can't be that hard. I'll be your John Watson."

"Wonderful," said Abigail. "And I'll be there to help you write them."

"I know you will, hun. That's the only thing that's putting me off."

"Huh. No one can say I've ever been accused of sticking my nose in when it's not wanted."

"Really?" said Hayley, quizzically.

"Well, not many," she said and smiled.

"Really?" said Terry and Betty together.

"Well, no one's said it today. Apart from you. Okay, I'll only help when you say I can. How's that?"

"It's a deal. I'm quite excited about it. I don't suppose it will ever get published, but who knows."

"You'd have to have a plum de noom, or whatever they call it," said Betty excitedly.

"That's a good idea, hun. I'll have a go tonight and see what I can come up with."

Betty put her arm through Terry's. "Come on, Terry. I'd much rather hear the story all about your meeting with Vera."

"My sister? That sounds so nice. Well, thanks to Hayley, we got to know each other quite a bit. We even like the same things. She told me that Alex and his family are coming over for Christmas and he's looking forward to meeting his cousins."

Abigail would much rather talk about murder. She knew

Terry was as happy as a dog with two tails, but he'd been talking about it for the last two days non-stop. She tried to change the subject. "Have they charged Christopher Briggs yet, Hayley?"

"Yes, they have. He folded like a pack of cards when they confronted him with it. Told them everything that he had done. Tom said he's like a haunted man. I'm wondering if that was literal. Veronica Stokes wasn't a very nice person in life, I should imagine she might be rather vengeful in death. He's in for a rough time, for sure. I reckon Hugh will be having a word with his mates behind bars as well. Cassie, of course, is heartbroken. She can't protect him now and will be jailed herself, so it was all for nothing. She had no idea that her beautiful boy could ever have committed such a horrific murder."

Betty shook her head, "Talk about rose-coloured tentacles."

"Oh, Betty," laughed Hayley. "I thought you said something else for a minute. I think you mean spectacles. Talking of mums, I'm going to Little Chortle to meet Sonia tomorrow. Suzie said she's still suffering. She can ask as many questions as she likes, and I'll try to give her some tips on how to relax. Her job as a social worker for children doesn't help. But what cases have we got left on the books, Abigail?"

"Well, we mustn't forget that man we met at your house who wanted to find his mother-in-law's jewellery. I'll go round to Mrs Goggins with Suzie later and have a look around, and hopefully, find the lady herself."

"It's not a case, but I really should call on Lady Fiona. She needs to know that the cat is well and truly out of the bag with her gambling."

"I think you mean horse," said Abigail.

"That's true. I know I can help. Trouble is, she'll probably shoot the messenger."

Betty laughed. "I hope not, dear. We've got enough cases as it is."

Terry added, "We sure have. I met a woman yesterday who's

coming to the library at midnight. She was killed in a car accident. Her brakes packed up when she came down Devils Hill. Now it might be wear and tear, but she's noticed her husband is a lot more friendly with their next-door neighbour than he ever let on. So I said we'll check them out. And this one's perfect for you, Hayley. A lovely man died two years ago and he wants you to tell his wife that it's okay if she marries his friend. He'd rather see her happy again than on her own."

"Now that's my kind of case. Very romantic for a change," said Hayley. "And talking about that, we're all dying to know what's going on with you two?"

Terry and Abigail looked at each other and he said, "So far we've had one date ending in a murder and a lovely walk on the downs, so early days."

"Romance and murder, I would have thought that was your dream date, Abigail," said Betty.

"I know, what a thoughtful man he is. But next time, Terry, can you arrange it after the quiz has finished? I was just about to beat Hayley."

"Never. We'd got every question right. The only one we had to guess was how many boiled eggs Cool Hand Luke ate."

"No, we didn't have a clue either, did we, Terry?"

Betty grinned. "I thought everyone knew that. He ate fifty eggs in one hour."

"You're an amazing woman, Betty," said Hayley, clapping. "I did not know that. You win the quiz then, hun."

"People think I haven't got my wits about me, but I hide my light under my bush, as they say."

"Oh, dear, Betty. You should have quit while you were ahead," laughed Abigail. "But well done. Now what else have we got coming up?"

"Don't forget it's nearly Wickers Night," said Terry.

"Oh yes," said Betty. "It comes round quicker each year."

Hayley was puzzled and Abigail said, "I remember that from

school. That's not real, is it? I thought it was just village folklore."

Terry said, "Of course it's real. It's a wonderful story. Emily Wickers was jilted on her wedding day in the 1700s. She threw herself into the village pond and drowned. And now every anniversary of her death, at midnight, she returns and entices men to their death. They see her in the water and when they reach out to help her, Emily grabs them and pulls them into the dark water to exact her revenge on the man that broke her heart and left her at the altar. Oh no, it's not a myth. Of course, it's been exaggerated over the years. The story now is that she took an axe to her fiancé and then the villagers drowned her. And that there's been at least a hundred men who have been drowned by her. When there may be three at most."

"Are you sure you're not having us on?" asked Hayley.

"As God is my witness," said Betty. "I've met her myself. She has mellowed over the years. She just haunts the village green now. But there was a young man in the nineties that drowned on Wickers Night, but that might have had something to do with the seven pints of best bitter he drank in the Cricketers. But it helped to keep the legend going. I think she shows herself to keep the tradition alive these days. I'll introduce you both if you like."

"Well, you learn something every day," said Abigail.

Hayley breathed in hard and told them something else they didn't know. "I've got another surprise for you all. I'm thinking of adding an advert on my website that I have for my psychic services. I'm thinking of offering help as a Private Detective. I might even call it The Deadly Detective Agency, with your help, of course."

They were all thrilled and Abigail clapped her hands and said, "Amazing, Hayley. A fabulous idea. You'll have even more things to write about. Don't take on anything dangerous though, will you? Otherwise, we might have to move into your house to protect you."

"Ah, I can't think of anything I would love... less," she joked, but meant it sincerely. "No, I promise. I've just realised that some people have problems that I can't help with as a faith healer or medium. Look at Fiona Cummings, she was being blackmailed and had nowhere to turn. If she had come to us, or me, maybe we could have stopped Dora from ruining her life. I'm hoping it won't be murders, just everyday problems."

"That's such a good idea," said Terry. "We can do the surveillance and Suzie can do the searches. At least we won't need a warrant."

"I'm so thrilled," said Betty. "I almost think we're cheating with all the special gifts we have. And you're like a human lie detector, Hayley. A private eye. I like the sound of that. Ooh, how about The Private Third Eye."

"I like it. Or Private Eyes of the Third Kind. So The Deadly Detective Agency will be truly opened for business. I'll get it up online as soon as I can. I'll write something like 'Discreet enquiries at excellent rates'. I'll have to charge something. But what I thought, if you're all in agreement, is that after I've paid myself a bit, I'd open a trust fund for Suzie's brother, Jordan. He's going to need money in a few years for university and that's not cheap." They all thought that it was a marvellous idea.

"If John could see me, he would be so proud," said Betty.

"He probably can, hun. I expect it will be small jobs like lost pets and cheating spouses, but a job's a job."

"I suppose I could check in the bedrooms if I had to," chuckled Betty, who at eighty-two had proven to be quite open to anything salacious!

"And no, Terry, you can't check on Rebecca Jones if the subject comes up," joked Abigail. "Make sure you do it all online then, Hayl. You don't want anyone turning up at your house at all hours."

"Definitely. I have enough of that with you lot. No, it will be all emails and then on my phone. I wonder what our first case will be."

"What I'd really like is a nice deadly murder."

"Hang on, Abi, it's Tom ringing. Hi... Yes... When?... Really?... I see... I'll call you later. Bye."

They all looked expectantly at her. "You won't believe this, but it sounds like you're in luck, Abi. Tom is on his way to another murder. I expect you've heard of the Ottersmill Regatta. Well, it's the last day today and they've just found a body in the river. Someone has been hit on the head and drowned."

"That's not necessarily murder," said Terry. "They could have fallen in the river and accidentally been hit by a racing crew. They go very fast at these things, and they probably wouldn't have even realised."

"Ah, the only problem with that is the weapon, or maybe it was an oar, was found on the riverbank with blood on it. It wasn't in the rowlocks."

"Thank goodness for that. Well, at least that's a blessing for the poor man. That would have been very painful," said Betty. Abigail stifled a laugh and had to wonder if Betty was actually a lot more clever and decidedly more funny than she let on.

"It might not be a man, Tom didn't say, did he? We better go and find out."

"Exactly. So who fancies a car ride to Ottersmill?" asked Hayley excitedly.

"Need you ask. And you'd better start writing, Hayley." said Abigail. "This one will be The Case of the Deadly Regatta."

THE END

About the Author

Ann Parker was born in Hertfordshire, England and still lives there with her husband, Terry, and her black and white cat, Jazz.

She is the author of the Abigail Summers Cozy Mysteries - The Deadly Detective Agency & The Case of the Deadly Pub Quiz, and the short story book entitled Magic & Memories. Ann has had poems published on Spillwords and in the bestselling anthology, Hidden in Childhood, as well as various magazines.

When she is not writing, she loves to spend time with her family or reading a good whodunnit.

To learn more about Ann Parker and discover more Next Chapter authors, visit our website at www.nextchapter.pub.

Printed in Great Britain
by Amazon